BRIDGEBREAKER

The Echo Worlds, Book 2

By: Joshua C. Cook

DEDICATION

To my Wife: Always

To my Friends and Family, Thank you for all your support and encouragement.

ACKNOWLEDGEMENT

Beta Readers:

James Hockney

Angelique M Keppler Bochnak

Nicole Kiefer

Table of Contents

Of what has come before 6

Chapter 1 9

Chapter 2 20

Chapter 3 33

Chapter 4 47

Chapter 5 55

Chapter 6 63

Chapter 7 72

Chapter 8 80

Chapter 9 91

Chapter 10 97

Chapter 11 105

Chapter 12 113

Chapter 13 126

Chapter 14 131

Chapter 15 143

Chapter 16 152

Chapter 17 158

Chapter 18 169

Chapter 19 180

Chapter 20 194

Chapter 21 206

Chapter 22 217

Chapter 23 225

Chapter 24 234

Of what has come before

Cendan Key is a man with a plan, a plan for everything. A plan for living, a plan for sleeping. He likes control, and knowing what is going to happen, and when. His life is thrown out of his plan when his well-organized life intersects with a creature from outside our World, Grellnot. Grellnot is the prime hunter of people with magical talent, it eats their power, absorbing it. And often eats the people as well.

For Cendan Key is far more than he appears, or even he knows. Cendan Key is born to be a Bridgefinder, an ancient organization fighting to defend our world from the Echo. The Echo world is ruled by a creature known only as the Slyph, and there she wields ultimate power, and can create life itself.

The Slyph wants to merge her world with ours, to control not only the magic of the Echo, but the barely used but strong magic of ours. Cendan finds himself thrown into the Bridgefinders, only to discover that they are a dying group, clinging to remnants of power, desperate to turn the tide of the war. Cendan gets an even greater shock when he discovers that not only is he a Bridgefinder, he's a Maker. Born with the special skills and talents needed to create incredible objects that bind magic into physical form.

The Bridgefinders down to three members, plus Cendan. Marcus, the erstwhile leader of the group. Jasmine, a woman with a surprising connection to Cendan, and Sal, a recent recruit himself. They have lost knowledge, and lost EVA, an intelligent machine. EVA was created by the last Bridgefinder Maker, known only as Oakheart. Eva can work near miracles in their war, but only a Maker can fix her.

Cendan tries to understand this world he's been thrown into, but wants to return to his old life. Only an outright attack by Grellnot causes him to rethink walking away. Grellnot discovers that it can't harm Cendan because of his Maker status, returns to the Slyph, angry and in pain. Meanwhile, Cendan knows he needs to understand what being a Maker truly means, decides that the only way to get information is going to be to travel to the Echo World himself, and find Oakheart. The last Maker of the Bridgefinders was captured by the Slyph over a millennium ago, but is somehow still alive.

Traveling there, he is intercepted by the Elves, who have fallen out of favor with the Slyph. They force Cendan into a bargain, a bargain that he will find a way for them to visit our world again, in exchange for their help getting to Oakheart. Cendan regrets this choice once he realizes that the Elves only want access to kidnap humans. Human women.

Cendan finds Oakheart, turned into a huge tree. The Slyph had been keeping him alive, using him as a conduit to draw what magic out of our world she could. Oakheart and Cendan find a way to communicate, and he shares what knowledge he still retains. Oakheart then stops fighting, and allows himself to die, robbing the Slyph of access to our world's power.

Grellnot finds Cendan on the Echo world, but Cendan is able to talk Grellnot into letting him go. The Slyph discovering this, having no more patience with Grellnot attempts to unmake him, and fails. Shaken, she banishes him to a deep dark cave, the same cave she was born into.

Grellnot however, having absorbed the power of multiple Bridgefinders is stronger than the Slyph knows. Its new powers allow it to start to eat the raw magic of the Echo world itself, something that had been denied to it before now.

The Slyph knowing that she is under threat from Grellnot launches her final attack, in an attempt to force the merge of the worlds now. The Bridgefinders work to repel her. Cendan and Sal stay behind, working to fix EVA before it's too late. The Slyph sends two special creatures through into the Bridgefinders headquarters to hunt and kill them both.

Sal sacrifices himself to give Cendan time to finish the repairs. Cendan is successful, and EVA is reborn. The tide turns quickly as the Slyphs' creatures are banished and bridges between their worlds are closed.

The Slyph and Grellnot now face off as enemies on the Echo World, while the rest of the Bridgefinders heal their wounds and rest, unsure of the what to do now, or where the Slyph will strike next.

Chapter 1

"Grellnot hungry," muttered Grellnot as it sniffed the air, searching for another meal. Pain shot through its stomach as it searched. Sniff-sniff; the air carried different scents to it, fire and smoke, old now, from the area where Oakheart once stood. The Slyph had not been happy when she had found out that human Maker had been there. Grellnot still wondered if it would have been better to have just eaten the stupid human. Grellnot had let it go.

Stupid Slyph had made Grellnot stronger, however. A wide smile broke out across Grellnot's face. Grellnot was far more now than he had ever been. Grellnot concentrated, and could see the weave of magic around him, the threads underlying everything nearby. These threads connected everything too, strong and thick to the rest of the world. Grellnot was different however; mixed with the weave were dots, points of bright light that only it could see. Grellnot knew that this was the magic of the human world, magic that was part of his creation, and the magic that he had absorbed from countless Finders and their shiny treasures.

One gnarled and clawed finger ran through the treasures around its neck, the musical chiming sound soothing to Grellnot. A fresh shot of pain arced across his stomach and Grellnot growled. Hungry; always hungry. Grellnot knew he could eat the magic raw, eat it and leave a hole in the very fabric of the world. Grellnot wanted blood though, blood and bone, magic and flesh. There, on the edge of his senses; goblins. Moving fast. Goblins were good eating to Grellnot. Tasty, not too tough, and more than willing to throw one of their number to appease his appetite.

Grellnot launched itself down the steep embankment that it had been perched on, moving in great leaps and bounds towards the roving band of goblins. A Stonemal, small and young, dove into the rocks to avoid Grellnot. It had no interest, however, in the small creature. Stonemals, while edible, were not to Grellnot's way of thinking very juicy. He could sense the goblin band getting closer when they suddenly changed direction, moving very decidedly away from Grellnot's approach.

With a low gurgle, Grellnot leaped into the air and forced itself to translate to where the Goblins were. One strange side-effect of its new power was that its old trick of translating to a new location had gotten harder. Grellnot was not sure why, but found it used more energy, which just made him even hungrier. Grellnot popped into existence directly in the path of the goblin band, exactly as it had planned.

The goblins were led by a larger than normal member of their race, who once it realized that Grellnot was there, immediately fell to the ground, prostrating in front of Grellnot.

"Do not eat us, Grellnot master. Scragin sorry Grellnot bothered by us." The goblin's voice was a cracking mess that set Grellnot's teeth on edge.

"Grellnot is hungry, goblin. Very hungry. There are nine goblins here. Grellnot will leave when there are eight." Grellnot eyed the band of goblin raiders. Dirty, but all decently sized, all good to eat. Their arms were bloody, at least some of them were; the iron rich smell of Baruz blood. "Been hunting Baruz?" Grellnot asked clicking his teeth. Which goblin to eat? The tall one there? Not much fat on it, but those long arms would have good bones to crunch. Or that end one, fatter than the rest, and the most scared to Grellnot's senses.

Yes, the one on the end stank of fear strongly. Delicious fear.

"Yes mighty Grellnot, the Baruz had struck at us so we attacked them back." Grellnot ignored him, eyeing that fat goblin more. Baruz and Goblins hated each other, anyway. Baruz were like goblins but were dark grey-blue, and usually smarter. They were also good eating, and for a second Grellnot thought about going to the Baruz camp and eating the dead and wounded. But they wouldn't be alive and afraid, and Grellnot wanted that fresh fear.

"That one; give Grellnot that one and the rest of you can live, stupid goblins." Grellnot pointed a finger at the fat goblin.

"Scumridge? You want Scumridge?" the lead goblin asked, hopeful that he wouldn't get eaten.

"Grellnot not care what its name is. It's tasty." Grellnot shot back, never taking its eyes off the fat goblin that was now quaking in fear. The other goblins moved away from it, the smell of relief rising off them.

"Take him!" the lead goblin yelled and hid its head. Grellnot leaped upon the poor creature, its hunger overpowering now. The fat goblin, Scumridge, gave one slight gurgling scream before the crunch of broken bones and the soft rip of flesh ended any sound it could make. The rest of the goblins turned and ran away as fast as they could. Grellnot, even while feasting, made a note of which way they went. Then it turned its attention to the task at hand; eating.

The Slyph paced in a circle, deep in thought. Her hounds followed her at a distance. For the first time in her long existence, she felt threatened. Firstly, the Bridgefinders had managed to not only find a new Maker, who against all odds had come here – here! – to her world, find Oakheart and somehow take him away from her. Not only that, but this new Maker, Cendan Key, had also been able to repair that damned machine, the EVA.

She had been so close to winning, to finally forcing a merger of the two worlds where she, the Slyph, would control both worlds and all the magic. She had been on the edge of winning her long war. But then the EVA had come back online, and nearly instantly everything had reversed. Her Bridges closed, and her creatures and creations were banished. Worse, the long years of work to carefully and slowly weaken the barriers between the two worlds had been tossed out the window since the EVA could now constantly strengthen it.

And to make matters worse, Grellnot, her one-time favorite hunter of Finders, had turned against her. Grellnot had absorbed enough magic, enough raw power, to put itself outside of her control. But the vile thing had done one worse too; it had learned how to eat the raw magic of this world, to rip it out and use it to slake its all-consuming hunger.

The hole left by the thing when it had eaten its way out of the cavern still felt like an open wound to the Slyph. She was part of the very fabric of the magic here, and the hole was just that a ripped hole in her mind. Damn that creature. It had been nearly two weeks now, earth weeks, and no sign of the creature, but she knew he was out there still.

Grellnot was the more immediate threat. The Bridgefinders were in fact just standing in her way; protecting their own. In a way she understood that, even as misguided and foolish as it was. Magic, all magic was hers by right, regardless of which world it was on or from. But at least the Finders weren't attacking her.

Nor were they a threat to the very world she had built and shaped.

But how to stop the beast that Grellnot had become? She couldn't unmake it. She had tried, and her failure to do so had shaken her to the core at the time. It was something she had never expected, to be stymied by one of her own creations. Grellnot was too powerful even then, but now things were worse. He was strong, infused with the power of two worlds, and as always very hungry. Sooner or later it would try to feed on her once it occurred to it to try.

Maybe that was the main edge she had, that Grellnot, for all its raw power and anger, wasn't very smart. Could she find a way to separate it from its power someway? Barring that, could a creature or creatures physically overpower and destroy the thing? Grellnot wasn't a large creature. Tough and strong, but not large.

A hound stuck its large head under her hand, and she scratched it absentmindedly, her fingers ruffling its loose and patchy fur. Her hounds were created the same way as Grellnot: partially of her world's magic and partially of the human world's magic; pulled through the now dead and gone Oakheart. She knew that to human eyes her hounds were abominations. Large four legged things, patchy fur and loose skin, with three large tentacles, one from each front shoulder and one in between the other two. Each of those tentacles had a large sharp bone ridge running down the middle of the last third.

Her hounds were loyal, strong, and unthinking. She should have used them from the start. They couldn't talk back, and wouldn't get ideas the way Grellnot had. Her hounds… The Slyph paused and looked at them. They weren't strong enough to take on Grellnot, at least not like this, but maybe with some changes... She was smiling, a smile of pure malice.

Cendan paused and stretched. He couldn't read another damn line in this book. The book, large and heavy, sat in front of him. The personal journal of the last Maker before him, encoded but deciphered with the knowledge that that same former Maker had somehow placed into Cendan's focus. It covered so many topics, and none of them in an organized way.

For Cendan, someone who found comfort and peace in a strict organization stand point, the book was maddening. It jumped around topics, and sometimes, even pages would be out of order. He had caught himself more than once wondering if he should find a way to transcribe the whole thing. Then he thought about how long that would take and thought better of it.

Reaching across the table, he slammed the book shut, listening to the echoes of the slap the book made as its heavy cover came down. Echoes. As in more than one echo. Jolting upright in his seat, Cendan knew he needed to find Marcus, and now.

Cendan quick-walked down the hallway, finally used to the semi random nature of the place. Part of it still bothered him, but when he got claustrophobic, he went to the Garden to unwind. He'd even started studying the Echo World plants there and making notes. Everything he'd seen when he had actually been there had looked the same as our world, minus some of the foodstuffs that the Elves had been eating.

Elves. Rubbing his head with his palms, Cendan still didn't know what to do about his deal with the Elves. Even more so after he realized what they were actually after. Could he actually ignore them? They were locked away on the Echo World after all. And since EVA came back online there hadn't been a single Bridge appear anywhere; at least according to the map.

EVA, Cendan thought in his head. They had quickly worked out a deal, him and EVA. She wouldn't talk into his head without him asking her to. He found it too strange and kind of creepy to have her there otherwise. He wasn't sure if she could see what he was thinking regardless of whether he wanted to talk, but he didn't want to find out.

"*Yes, Cendan?*" EVA's voice echoed in his head still. "*What do you need?*" Her tone was one of amusement to his mind.

"What makes you think I need something? Can't I just say Hi?"

EVA came back quickly, "*Cendan. We've been merged for a little over two weeks, and if there's one thing I already know about you, you're not one to ever just say hi.*" There was a pause. "*If you're looking for the others, Jasmine is out and Marcus is in the barrier room as usual.*"

Still beating himself up over Sal's death probably, Cendan knew. Sal had died trying to stop those damn dog-like creatures of the Slyph's. They had been fixing the damage done to EVA, or at least working around it, when the Slyph had made her move. A full out invasion of the human world. Marcus and Jasmine had gone out to stop what they could while he and Sal worked to being EVA back online. What they hadn't known was that she had sent two new creatures after them, hound like things, and gotten them here into the headquarters.

Cendan quickly found his way to the barrier room to find Marcus once again sitting in his favorite chair, staring at the board in front of him. The board held spaces for hundreds of foci, if not a thousand, but now only two were in use; his and Marcus's. Jasmine's was with Jasmine, wherever she was at the moment. Rule of thumb; if you leave the lair, bring your focus.

"Marcus, got a moment? I have a question; something occurred to me and you of anyone here might know the answer." Cendan awaited Marcus's response. Since Sal's death, Marcus had retreated to this room every day. Earth was safer now than it had been in over a thousand years, with EVA back on the job. But still, Marcus was the leader of a pitiful band of what once was thousands.

"What is it Cendan." Marcus didn't turn to look at him.

"Well, I was wondering. Are there any other echo worlds? I mean, a sound has more than one echo, so if our world has an echo, wouldn't there be more than one?" Cendan asked.

Marcus shifted in his seat and Cendan winced. Always touchy about certain subjects, Marcus took being a Bridgefinder deadly seriously.

However, Marcus refused to believe that what they did was magic, in any sense of the word. He rejected the thought. Sal had been more open to the idea, but he was not here anymore. Jasmine had also rejected the idea, at least at first. Both she and Marcus had healed somewhat from their injuries during the Slyph's assault, and during that time Jasmine had asked him some quiet questions about magic.

Marcus, however, clung to his prejudice. What made it all the more galling to Cendan was that the refusal to accept what they did as magic, or even the far greater things they could do, was all borne of a fringe belief of a small faction of Bridgefinders long ago. Somehow the idea had taken over, though, and the Bridgefinders had turned their backs on a large amount of their power.

"Why do you ask? Still looking for proof of your magic idea?" Marcus asked in return, his voice low and tired.

"No, just something that occurred to me when I closed Oakhearts journal. I heard the echo of the book slamming closed, and it just occurred to me..." Cendan trailed off.

"The answer is, we don't know. Or least I don't know. The question has been asked before, more than once. I will say that we've only had evidence of one echo that connects to our world. If there are others, they don't seem to connect to our world; at least directly."

Suddenly Marcus stood and walked toward Cendan. His face, always sharp edged, looked haggard now, drawn. "Your books in the Maker wing may have more information."

Marcus stopped in front of Cendan and spoke. "What I'm more interested in is why there hasn't been a single bridge formed in the last two weeks. Nothing. Not even the rare outlier. It's as if there isn't a single connection between the worlds, though we know there still are – the map says so. But the Slyph hasn't tried. Even once. Why?"

Cendan shrugged. In truth, he wondered why as well. EVA has told him that she hadn't had to even try to stop anything, and for the last two weeks she'd been strengthening the barrier twenty-four hours a day with no interference from the other side. She seemed pretty damn happy about it as much as a clockwork contraption could be.

"I don't know. Is that really a problem though? Maybe she's trying to figure out what to do next. Maybe she's hurt or injured. Or maybe she's given up. Who cares? All that really matters is that she's not attacking us, right?" Cendan sat down in a chair covered with golden leaves. "Let's just enjoy the peace while it lasts."

A snort was Marcus's only reply at first. Shoulders hunched, Marcus stalked toward the door to leave the barrier room.

"Peace? Cendan, there is no peace, ever. One way or another this is all going to have to end." Marcus paused and turned toward Cendan, his eyes sunken and his voice even more worn than normal. "You don't get it do you? At first, when you brought that machine back online, the one in your head, I was happy. Ecstatic even. For the first time in an unknown number of years, we were going to be gaining ground. Or so I thought. But Sal died. You lived. That got me thinking. What would happen if you died? Would EVA keep working? Would it stop all over again? There are now just three of us left, Cendan. Three."

Cendan didn't have an answer for him. Truthfully he'd never considered it, what would happen if he died? Before he could ask EVA, Marcus continued speaking.

"Cendan, Jasmine and I are the last of the born and raised Bridgefinders. We are it. You, while a Maker, didn't grow up in this. You didn't have it drilled into you day in and day out just how hard this fight is. Sal didn't either. It's one reason he's dead. I should have made sure he understood that losing even one of us is far too many."

"And you... Cendan, you don't understand any of it. You mock our traditions, push us to things that are out of bounds, want us to believe in things that can't be true. Magic? Other worlds besides the Slyph's? You treat this like a game. This is for the very damn survival of the species, and all you can think of is hypothetical nonsense!" Marcus spat the last words at Cendan, leaving him surprised at the venom behind them.

"You brought us a reprieve, Cendan, but I wish beyond measure that you hadn't come to the Red Orchid that day. That Grellnot hadn't found you when he did. I wish you'd never become one of us. I thought having a Maker would fix so many problems, but all it's done is give us a breather at the cost of what it means to be a Bridgefinder." Grimacing, Marcus paused, his mouth snapping shut and his eyes shooting a look of hate that surprised Cendan to the core.

The door to the Barrier room slammed behind him as Marcus left, leaving Cendan to stare at the board himself and wonder what was coming next.

Chapter 2

Jasmine was happy though still somewhat in pain. Her fingers rubbed her scalp, feeling the short sharp hairs starting to grow, even as she avoided touching the healing blisters at her hairline. She knew she looked somewhat terrifying still to people though. Normal people that is. Her running excuse of a car accident that she used when pressed on what happened seemed to mollify the curious though.

Grocery buying wasn't the most glamorous part of being a Bridgefinder. Really, though, they had to eat. She mentally checked off her list, trying hard not to think about the items missing, the one's Sal would have wanted. Sal. Earnest and friendly, and truly out of his league on things. Sal had never been powerful in skill. In the past he'd never have been a Bridgefinder, but these days they took anyone who had the ability.

A deep sigh escaped her as Jasmine thought about the newest member, Cendan. In her heart, she still had trouble putting him in as a Bridgefinder. And not just any Bridgefinder, but a Maker. The first Maker in over a thousand years, and he had to be an ex. An ex that she couldn't even begin to make sense of. Still attractive, but hard headed. Talented and an amazing mind, but still not really plugged in emotionally. There had been some movement in that direction though; he'd grown some.

Jasmine was still ruminating about the state of her relationship with Cendan when her cart banged against another shopper's.

"Oh sorry! Wasn't looking where I was going," she called out before locking eyes with the other shopper. It was a young woman, attractive enough looking, except for her hair which was red with a long streak of blue. The eyes, though, locked onto her and she couldn't move.

Goosebumped arms and the tingle down her spine at first confused her, but then with growing awareness she knew. This woman had the power. She was one of those outsiders that she had long been warned of.

Bridgefinders had long been aware of those few humans who could see and understand the Bridges between this world and the echo. The few who could do so, but yet weren't Bridgefinders, and in fact would deal with the creatures of the Slyph in return for power and knowledge. Officially they were thought of as almost misguided children. Marcus found them disgusting, but Marcus was full of prejudice these days.

Jasmine found herself unable to speak, and a weak croak was all she could manage as she tried to say something. Eyes narrowing, the other woman gave a small nod, and left, pushing her cart away slowly. Jasmine tried to follow but was stuck to the spot, her legs also not wanting to obey her. A few minutes later her voice returned; a croak escaped her. Pins and needles rushed up her legs, as if they had been asleep, cut off from circulation.

She tried to find the other woman, but she was gone as far as Jasmine could tell, and her legs were still weak; wobbly. She grabbed a bottle of water from her cart and opened it, drinking it down while trying to figure out what had just happened. Why would one of the others, the outsiders, a witch if you wanted to call her that, come here? Come here and find her?

There was no doubt this hadn't been an accident. Those who dealt with the Echo weren't welcome here and hadn't been for an extremely long time. It hadn't been a formal agreement, not a grand sit down and signing of a treaty, but many generations ago, those outside the Bridgefinders found it better and safer for them to not be here. There was a lot of resentments too, over EVA, since EVA could act as a sort of Bridge magnet that limited those outside of the Bridgefinders from gaining access to the Echo world and its creatures.

That had led to the slow reduction of those who claimed to be witches and warlocks, wizards and soothsayers. Normal people, those who knew nothing of the Echo, just thought that the stories had just died off; that enlightenment and knowledge had eventually ended the superstitions of the old eras. But the truth was that the Bridgefinders had cut them off from their power for the most part, and so they had died off.

This of course made for a highly frosty relationship. Sure, the occasional Bridge could form outside the influence of EVA. Rumors had come sometimes of ways to form a Bridge from this world to the Echo world. Those stories had always been treated as rumors and lies by the Bridgefinders, though in light of Cendan's recent proclamations about magic, maybe they shouldn't have been.

Jasmine continued to look for the woman as she shopped, but didn't see a sign of her anywhere, and in fact the rest of the shopping trip continued without incident. Leaving the store and loading her car, Jasmine kept feeling like she was being watched, however; that prickling on the back of the neck; the slight tension in the air. But glancing around she saw nothing.

Returning the cart to the store, she was just about to get in her car when a voice came from behind her.

"So you're a Bridgefinder, huh? I'm not impressed."

Jasmine whirled around to see the same woman from inside the store standing there; same red hair; same blue streak. The only thing different this time was what she was holding. A wooden circle, twisted almost. One look at it and Jasmine knew: that was a focus. Who was this woman?

"Excuse me?" Jasmine decided to play dumb. "Bridgefinder? I'm sorry, I don't know what you're talking about. Now if you will excuse me—"

"Your name is Jasmine Wanatabi. You're a seventh generation Bridgefinder. You use a red orchid to concentrate your abilities. It's your fetish, your tool." The woman continued. "And right now you all, what's left of the *mighty* Bridgefinders, don't have a damn clue as to what's going on."

Jasmine paused. How did the woman know that much about them? Realization came quickly. She used the word fetish, not focus; she's a witch. One of those people who could be Bridgefinders, but instead used their abilities to help themselves, furthering their power. An anathema to the Bridgefinders and everything that they stood for. What was she doing? And what was she doing here?

"Your kind isn't welcome here, witch," Jasmine shot back. "Take your attitude and go back to whatever hole you crawled out of. You betray your world and want me to listen to you?" Jasmine's anger rose quickly. "We have beaten back the Slyph for the first time in centuries. Soon your little power plays will be over."

Laughter erupted from the other woman. "As I expected from a Bridgefinder. An overly righteous better-than-you tone, and flat-out missing the point." The other woman took a step closer to jasmine. "My name is Heather. And yes, I'm a witch. I'm here because, as much as your kind make me angry, you all deserve to know what's coming. You may have won a battle against the Slyph, you and that ... machine."

Jasmine noted Heather's grimace when she mentioned the machine, EVA. How did the witch know about that? Heather continued, however, breaking Jasmine's train of thought.

"But things have changed on the Echo World and changed in a big way. The Slyph is still a danger, but there is a much larger one now."

Jasmine snorted. "There's nothing we need from you, witch. I don't care what your name is, and I don't care why you are here. The day you and yours are gone from this world, the better." Deciding to ignore the woman and get back to the headquarters to talk this over with Marcus, Jasmine got in the car, quickly checking over the supplies.

"Foolish woman. I came here because I thought maybe the Bridgefinders would want to know that Grellnot, the killer of so many of your kind, is now in open rebellion on the Echo world. There's a war brewing between the Slyph and Grellnot, and if Grellnot wins, you're not just going to have to deal with the merging of the worlds. You will also have a creature who wants to see each and every damn living thing on both worlds' dead and devoured, sacrificed to its hunger." Heather stood in front of the car, anger flashing in her eyes.

Jasmine paused. Grellnot and the Slyph were at war? The thought of Grellnot having all the power of the Echo world at its disposal was a terrifying one. Jasmine cocked an eye at the witch.

"How do you know this? One of your creatures tell you?"

Heather nodded. "Yes. And I have a message for one of your members as well. One called Cendan Key."

Eyes wide, Jasmine raced into thought. None of this made sense, but she needed more information.

"What's the message?" Her thoughts turned towards Cendan, now. Why was he getting messages from the Echo world? What had he done there?

"Take me to him. The message is for him only." Arms crossed, the witch glared at Jasmine. Her focus, or fetish as she liked to call it, was still firmly gripped in her hand. Jasmine was unsure what to do. If this Heather person was correct, this was vital information to them. If she was lying, there was some kind of reason for it. Then there was Cendan. How did she know him, even his name?

Add to all that the fact that she had done something to Jasmine in the store… More and more, she knew that Cendan had been correct. Bridgefinders had powers they weren't aware of. They could do far more than just close Bridges and banish creatures back to the echo world. Marcus didn't even want to hear the idea said out loud and still reacted angrily to it. Jasmine had agreed with him for a long time, but things had been changing.

If she brought Heather to the headquarters, Marcus would be angry; probably very. But if she brought the young witch to the outside, and brought Cendan out to meet with her, that might work.

"Ok, I'll take you to a place where you can meet with Cendan. Don't try anything though." Jasmine's eye's flicked to the fetish in the witch's hand.

"As if you could stop me. I can feel your power, you know. You're full of it. Wasted ability; wasted power. You could be so much more than ... this ... door closer you've allowed them to make you." Her face plastered with a smirk, Heather got into the car beside her. "Don't worry, I won't do anything. The bit in the store was to get your attention. Harmless hold pattern ... or I guess you would say spell. Nothing to worry about."

Jasmine didn't answer. That had been a harmless spell? She found herself wondering what things would have been like if she'd made the witch actually angry. She also couldn't help wondering if she could replicate what the witch had done. Jasmine didn't talk during the drive; she didn't want to give anything away to her passenger. Heather, on the other hand, hummed a tune that Jasmine didn't know. It was a sort of ghostly tune; haunting; sad. Jasmine could feel the song almost taking her concentration away from driving. Thankfully it was a short drive to the Red Orchid. It was almost a relief to pull in and stop the car.

"You wait here. I'll talk to Cendan and see if he can, or wants, to come out." Jasmine pointed at the witch.

"What, you don't want me to help with the bags?" Eyes rolling, the young witch sighed. "Fine, I'll stay here."

Jasmine got as many bags as she could carry and descended the stairs to the transition point under the Red Orchid. She fumbled for a moment with the bags and her focus, but finally got the portal to home open.

Quickly she stepped inside and closed the door behind her. Jasmine walked quickly towards the kitchen, hoping she'd not given anything away to the witch. Find Cendan quickly, let him know what was going on, and don't let Marcus know. At least not yet. It pained her to keep things from Marcus; they'd known each other for a very long time. They'd practically grown up together in the Bridgefinders. Marcus had always craved the leadership of the organization, and had, when younger, been convinced that he would lead the group back to power and win the war with the Slyph. And in a way he had, but it had been Cendan who had actually done it.

Marcus was proud, and she knew he struggled with the fact that Cendan had been the pivotal person, not he. He and Cendan already had a delicate relationship, and the death of Sal had just put more strain on it all. Marcus still blamed himself for Sal's death, but also felt that Cendan could have done more, should have done more, to save him.

The kitchen was well lit and thankfully empty. If Cendan wasn't here, he might be in the Garden or in the Maker wing. Quickly, Jasmine put away the supplies, casting glances at the door and making sure she didn't miss him walking by. She also didn't want to keep that witch waiting too long. Heather didn't strike Jasmine as someone who had a great deal of patience.

Finishing up, Jasmine headed towards the Garden, hoping that Cendan was in there first. It was closer, and Marcus rarely went there. If she had to go to the Maker wing, that meant passing right by the barrier room, Marcus's favorite place to brood. Marcus, if he was in there, would want to know why she hadn't put her focus back right away as protocol dictated. Explaining why, that there was a witch outside wanting to talk to Cendan, was not something she wanted to do.

The doors to the Garden stood before her, green and ornate as always. She actually rather liked this place as-well, truthfully. The rest of the headquarters was very closed in. The Garden gave them a place to relax in the safety of the headquarters. Though not as safe apparently as they had all thought; the Slyph had managed to get two creatures in, the ones that had killed Sal. Cendan and EVA had said that the hound things were like Grellnot in a way, combinations of the magic of the Echo world and their world, which was why the protections in place hadn't kept them out.

Pushing open the doors, she felt relieved. Cendan was there, t-shirt and shorts, doing something with plants. His back was to the door, and he didn't seem to be paying too much attention. Jasmine couldn't help but notice that the few weeks he had been here had changed him. Not only mentally, but physically as well. He'd filled out a bit, and she found herself somewhat surprisingly appreciating the view she was getting.

Jasmine shook her head. They were just friends now. That part of their relationship was long gone and buried. And it was for the better. Cendan was a nice guy, a great guy, but his total tone deafness on emotions and any connection to people really drove her to distraction. There had been too many arguments about things that should have been obvious to anyone with any sort of awareness about feelings.

"Cendan. Got a minute?" Jasmine called out to him. Cendan glanced behind him and smiled.

"Hey Jasmine! Looks like you're healing up well." And he meant it. Her burns, once pretty bad looking, had really started to heal up. Her hair was going to obviously take a lot longer to recover. "Yeah, can you give me about fifteen minutes? I want to finish transplanting this... Well whatever it is." He gestured towards the plant in front of him, some kind of fruit plant with a strange almost pure cylindrical fruit that was blue fading to near black.

Jasmine shook her head. "Sorry, I kind of need you now. And … I don't want Marcus to find out what I need to talk to you about. Or show you."

Cendan gave her a much more appraising look. Jasmine wasn't one to hide things from anyone. Hiding something from Marcus was as about as out of character as he could imagine. Two things stood out to him now that he was paying attention: firstly, she was nervous. Her feet were moving a bit, and her left hand was finger tapping on her thigh. And secondly, her mouth was tight. She was more than nervous he realized; almost apprehensive, anxious even.

"What's going on, Jasmine? You never hide anything from anyone." His voice betrayed his concern. Things weren't right here, and he wasn't sure why. "Why can't Marcus know?"

Jasmine rolled her eyes and sighed. "Look, just come with me and I'll explain as we walk. I don't want to leave this going on longer than it needs to."

Cendan hesitated. This was all damn strange.

"Just trust me, ok Cendan. I just need to show you…" Jasmine trailed off, unsure of how to say that she needed him to come with her to meet a witch who can perform magic; who was here to warn them about Grellnot and the Slyph; and who had a special message just for him. "Just come on." Jasmine whirled around and fast walked out of the Garden.

Cendan stood for a moment, at a loss for what to do. This was odd. "EVA? Do you know what's going on?" Cendan had slowly gotten more comfortable talking to the presence in his head that was EVA. He still didn't want her 'there', all the time. He wasn't sure he'd ever want that.

"Not fully Cendan. I know she just came back into the headquarters, and there is something odd about her. There is a residue for the lack of a better term, of magic around her. I'm trying to identify."

Magic? Cendan startled. He'd better follow her, something was going on. He quickly walked after her, talking to EVA in his head as he chased after Jasmine.

"What do you mean magic? Jasmine cast a spell or something?" That would be beyond strange, as Jasmine, like Marcus, still at least nominally believed that Bridgefinders couldn't do magic, even though Cendan knew that wasn't the case at all.

"No Cendan, I believe that someone cast a spell on her. I don't know what it did, but I can say with some certainty that it's not in effect now. It's just residue, like fog on a mirror."

Cendan blanched a bit at this. Someone cast a spell on Jasmine? Who? What? How? Too many questions, too many branches. He needed more information, and the only way he was going to get it was to find and follow her.

"Hey EVA, stay with me. Not sure where this is going, but stay... aware, or whatever you want to call it when you're actively inside my head." He was sure that EVA was amused by that thought,

"Yes Cendan, I will. I wouldn't be too concerned, however, with Jasmine. As I said, it was residue. Not anything active."

"You say that, but someone casting a spell on us? Using magic, on one of us? And remember, we haven't had a bridge form in weeks." Cendan spied Jasmine, pacing by the exit of the lair. "Just stay aware, ok?"

EVA didn't answer directly though a feeling of comfort washed over him. Cendan still wasn't sure exactly how he felt about

EVA being in his head. On one hand she was powerful, intensely so, and pretty much joined to him permanently. Sometimes she was motherly and comforting. Other times she was all business.

Though since EVA was pretty much unique in the world, a magic steam punk AI isn't something you run down to the store and put on layaway. Who knew what or how she would react to things.

Finally, he caught up to Jasmine, who was still pacing and agitated. Pushing his inner conversation about EVA off to the side, Cendan tried to see the residue that EVA was talking about. He was getting better with this skill, the seeing of magic. And there it was, a faint covering of the multicolored dots that made up the magic of this world. Jasmine herself could work magic, but this didn't come from her. It smelled wrong.

He wasn't sure why he thought it smelled, but it did. It didn't have a bad feeling, just foreign, not of who Jasmine was.

"Jasmine, what's going on? You're acting strange," Cendan asked. His arms crossed, he looked at her face, trying to figure out where this was all going. "You want me to see something outside? And Marcus can't know? This is weird Jasmine, really weird."

Her head tilted to one side, and she winced. "I know Cendan, just come with me. You need to come with me."

Cendan paused, but nodded. He trusted her, how could he not? He'd followed her into the Red Orchid about a month ago, and here he was, member of a secret group tasked with protecting the world from magical creatures and their leader, who wanted to both drain all the Bridgefinders of magic, and merge the two worlds into one under the leadership of the Slyph. A thin smile formed on his face. Maybe it might be better not to trust Jasmine, considering how the last time worked out. He was, however, as protected as he could be right now; EVA in his head and active, and his focus in his pocket. He was loath to leave it in the Barrier room and had been ever since the attack. One more point of contention with Marcus.

Jasmine took her focus out of her jacket pocket and held it up as the barrier that marked the exit melted away. With a nod, they stepped through and were transported to the bottom of the stairs at the back of the Red Orchid restaurant. Cendan still found himself holding his breath when he went through that thing. It just still felt wrong to him. Crossing who knows what amount of distance – if that was even the scale he should be using – in a blink of an eye was a weird feeling.

Jasmine hurried up the stairs, not looking back at him. With a deep breath and release, Cendan followed. There, at the top of the stairs, was one of their cars, and a young woman was leaning against it, bored. She was playing with strange wooden circle that sort of looked twisted. Her head jerked towards them when Cendan felt it. Magic. Strong magic.

Chapter 3

The magic washed over him, coming from this woman! Reacting more than thinking, Cendan drew through his focus and slammed back against the tide, assisted by the presence of EVA in his head. The woman's eyes widened, and just as suddenly the magic stopped flowing from her. Cendan could see it, however, surrounding her, dense and flowing around the small hoop in her hand. It was a focus! Or something like it.

"So you're Cendan. I'm surprised. I didn't think your kind knew magic or what to do with it.." The woman's voice was pleasant enough, but the mocking tone set his teeth on edge.

Cendan turned toward Jasmine, "Please tell me there is a good reason for this?"

Jasmine struggled for a moment before the other woman cut in.

"Oh don't blame her. She has, or I should say had, a light geas set upon her when I held her down at the supermarket. She had to go get you." The woman held out a hand to shake Cendan's. "My name is Heather. Heather Anston. And I believe you know what I am."

Cendan eyed her and her hand. "You're a witch."

Heather nodded, her red hair making a halo in the breeze.

"Exactly that, Cendan Key. Now don't be rude, shake my hand."

He felt it then; a pull; a tug. An inner feeling started saying shake her hand, don't be rude, you don't want to be rude to her do you? Before he knew it, his right hand was a quarter of the way up before EVA's voice cut in, strong.

"Cendan! She's trying to lay a compulsion on you."

Cendan shuddered, and slowly lowered his hand, making a fist to fight the urges.

"Stop that. I will not be controlled, not by you."

Heather gave him an appraising look. "Very well. But I wonder if you'd be able to do that without that machine in your head. Oh don't look so surprised, I can feel it in there."

Cendan's face betrayed his surprise at the witch's apparent knowledge of EVA.

"How did you know about that?" he blurted out.

The witch, Heather, sighed and pushed her still unruly hair behind her ears.

"What is it with you Bridgefinders? You think the rest of us with the gift don't keep a very close eye on you all? Your little club, running around, trying to stop the Slyph. Instead of trying to win her over again, and have her like us, you run around poking your finger in her proverbial eye. And now, you all pushed her too far, and she got angry."

Heather paused and looked at Cendan square in the eye. "More to the point you made her angry, Cendan. She lost it, and she pushed too hard, and now something very bad has happened. The Slyph and Grellnot are at war. You all think that the worst that could ever happen is the Slyph winning. She just wants the magic that's all. If you all could have worked with her, found a way, none of this would have happened. Grellnot would have never been created; the Bridgefinders wouldn't even be a thing.

Hell, magic itself could have been something the world celebrated." Her voice louder now, she pointed at Cendan.

"But No! Your kind had to piss her off. Grellnot is no longer under her control. He's absorbed too much magic; he's grown. And you think the Slyph is bad? Grellnot is a thing of pure hunger; pure anger. He's the true threat. I came to warn you all. For all your blame in this fiasco, you Bridgefinders are users of the gift, even if you don't acknowledge it." Heather dropped her hand and looked down. "Fools you may be, but powerful ones nonetheless."

Heather glanced at Cendan with hooded eyes.

"I also have a message for you, Cendan Key. Lachnin sends his regards and reminds you; bargains made must be bargains kept." Silence enveloped them then; Jasmine, Cendan and the witch Heather.

Cendan felt one of those moments when time seemed to stop. He could almost feel the air thicken as his mind went into overdrive. Lachnin? The Elf King? How? Glancing at Jasmine, she gave him a blank expression. He wasn't sure she even knew what to say at this point. Her view of everything, what he assumed she had already started to question, had now been shattered. Magic could be done, it worked, and she knew in her heart that everything they had been taught, everything that she'd grown up believing, wasn't fully the truth.

He looked at Heather again. The witch's face had a smirk on it; she'd been waiting for this moment, to smack him with the fact that the Elves were waiting, watching. He'd made the bargain, but that had been before he knew the truth; that the Elves needed humans, and in particular, human women. There couldn't be more Elves without them. Forcing himself to take a deep breath, he stared-down Heather, careful not to let his momentary panic cross his face.

"I haven't forgotten." Cendan replied, more bitterly than he meant to. He opened his mouth to retort when a thought occurred to him. How did she know?

There'd been no bridges formed anywhere, according to the map, for two weeks, so how could this witch know about his bargain?

"The more important question is how do you know about my bargain with Lachnin and the Elves?" Cendan asked. He could still feel EVA's presence in the back of his mind; it was actually comforting to know that there was something or someone there to keep him protected.

"What do you mean? They told me. Well, they sent me a message at least." Heather looked confused. "You know, through a Bridge. They can't come through due to the ban by the Slyph, but they can send messages." She took one look at his face and Jasmine's, and knew something was off. "Why does this surprise you? Bridges form. You know this. Fewer outside this town thanks to that damn machine of yours, but they still form."

Jasmine cleared her throat to answer. "There's been no Bridges formed in the last two weeks at all, not since the attack by the Slyph. We'd know."

Cendan nodded in agreement. "Try again, Heather the Witch, how do you know?"

Heather laughed. "You've got to be kidding me. I was in contact with someone just last night. Here in this city."

Cendan and Jasmine exchanged looks of alarm. Cendan could usually tell if someone was lying, and she didn't appear to be.

"EVA, what do you think?" He mentally reached out to the system.

"Cendan, my abilities to detect Bridges and move them here is saying she's wrong. Everything I can sense says that no Bridges have formed from the Echo world at all." There was a pause as if EVA was trying to figure this out.

Cendan queried her quickly. "How does the detection work? I thought the map did that?"

"It does, I'm connected to the map." EVA answered back. *"We are tied together, in a way. Loosely tied. I get the information from the map and use that to 'steer' the Bridges here."*

Cendan mused as the others looked at him. The map. The leaves. Leaves!

"EVA, when the attack happened, Sal, and I ran into the map room to see leaves all over the floor. This was after the hounds got in..."

EVA answered back, *"Cendan there is a chance that the map has been compromised. If so, we've been running blind for the last two weeks. We literally don't know what's been happening."*

Cendan ignored Heather and looked at Jasmine. "Jasmine, we have a problem. EVA thinks, and I agree, that the map may be broken. Or at least compromised." Jasmine's eyes shot up, but she nodded. "If so, we've got problems. But how would we know?"

Heather broke in. "You people really do know nothing. I can tell you if it's been modified, someway. Hell, I'll even show your boy wonder here how to do it himself, since he at least seems to know a bit more about how magic actually works."

Cendan waved Jasmine over to talk in confidence. Heather rolled her eyes and leaned back against the car, feigning disgust.

"EVA, can you tell if she's listening in?" Cendan asked.

"I'm not sure, but she's doing something. I can try to interfere, but I make no promises. This is strange." EVA responded. A few seconds later, Heather's hand shot up to her forehead, and just as quickly, she lowered it, shooting Cendan bird as she did so.

"I don't think she's listening in now, Jasmine." Cendan lowered his head until they were nearly touching. "What do you think? You brought her here."

Jasmine nodded. "Mostly against my will it appears, with that geas of hers on me. But it's true, if the map was modified or broken in some way by the creatures that broke in, the same ones that killed Sal, we've got a huge issue."

Cendan nodded. "My issue is that I don't know if we should let her, a self-professed witch, a user of magic, and a partner, if not servant, of creatures from the Echo World, look at the map." Jasmine kept speaking, quietly. "Then there's Marcus. If he knew we were talking to her, even right now, he'd blow his top. But bringing her into the headquarters? Showing her the map? That's even more dangerous."

Cendan knew she was right; they didn't know Heather and her helpfulness was, at best, suspicious. Marcus would go crazy if he found her in the lair, and after his earlier run in with Marcus, this would be one hell of an escalation of that fight. Jasmine wasn't aware of the run in that he'd had with Marcus earlier, but he wasn't sure about telling her. Marcus and Jasmine were close, not in a romantic way, but close. Setting them against each other would not be helpful, or at least he thought so. People; so damn strange to his way of thinking. Always bringing emotions into decisions.

Emotions had their place of course, and it wasn't like Cendan didn't feel them. Hell, he felt them quite strongly. But his got in the way when it came to decisions. People had asked if he was autistic or had Obsessive Compulsive Disorder at times, not really understanding what they were asking. Cendan was neither; he just refused to let emotional responses get involved when he had to make up his mind. He wasn't some character out of a science fiction show either. He'd heard that one more than once as-well. He had feelings, but he seemed to be able to put them to the side. So no, leave the more heated response he'd gotten from Marcus out of this for now. Concentrate on this issue; this witch looking at the map.

They had the cons of letting her in, but the pros were simple. Heather knew magic far better than he did. He'd been piecing it together from various notebooks and mentions in the Maker wing, but didn't understand half of it. Heather, though, had grown up with magic. She knew it the same way he knew the logical production methods for optimal efficiency. It would take him a lot of study and time to get even close to where he could be with an actual tutor. And the immediate problem; the map was super important. If the map was in fact broken then flying blind, as they were, could be deadly.

"I know how dangerous it is. I don't know…" Cendan paused and stared at the floor.

Jasmine jumped in. "Cendan, we need proof first. I'm willing to do this and start the fight of all fights with Marcus if you can prove to me the map is broken." Jasmine eyed Heather and

Heather glared back. "I don't trust her. I don't even like her, but I'm not sure if that's my bias talking or a gut instinct. I'll back you, but I want proof."

Cendan nodded. He had to keep in mind that Jasmine had been raised as Marcus had: to think nothing good of those who they called witches and wizards, warlocks, sorcerers, witch-doctors, and mediums. Indeed, anyone who dealt with the Echo World, who used the creatures and the powers there for personal gain and prestige. Add in the fact that this particular witch had very temporarily paralyzed her and then cast a geas – a magical compulsion to make Jasmine take her here - to the headquarters – and it was easy to understand where Jasmine was coming from.

Heather had been smart to use the geas. Cendan vaguely remembered reading that in folklore you couldn't force the person under a geas to go too far, which was why she hadn't tried to force Jasmine to get her inside. Push too hard and the geas breaks, like all those hypnotic suggestion things. You could suggest they stop smoking, or overeating, but try to get them to attack someone and it wouldn't work; pushed too far.

"Ok, we will make her prove it. But how? Form a Bridge here? Can that even be done? And then have us go look at the map?" Cendan asked confused.

Jasmine shrugged. "Yeah, I guess; I mean..." Jasmine's face lit up. "Hey, our phones don't work as phones in the headquarters, right? But that doesn't mean I can't record the map while she's doing whatever here. That way, we can both see it live, and then see the footage of the map. What about EVA? Can it check as well?"

Cendan nodded. "Yeah, she can." A quick mental ask – "Right?" – to EVA, followed up with only felt like a thumbs up, confirmed the thought. Though, with a touch of amusement, as Jasmine continued to call EVA an 'it'.

"Ok, we have a plan. Let's get proof first, and then if so, we can let her see the map, regardless of what the brooding boss has to say about it."

Approaching Heather, Cendan noticed that, for all her attitude, she was a remarkably attractive woman. Flaming natural red hair, except for that blue streak; grey eyes; pretty.

EVA poked him, *"Be careful, Cendan. There's enough magic swirling around her that I'm not sure what she's doing. I can't tell if she even really looks that way."*

Mentally shaking himself, Cendan looked Heather in the eye, receiving an arched eyebrow and a slight upturned smile in return. Red lips, those. Cendan wondered what it would be like to…

"Stop," he croaked out.

Heather laughed. "Stop what?"

Cendan fought his attraction and forced his eyes closed. That was better; he could think now.

"We want proof. Prove that the Bridges can still be open and the map doesn't see it, and we will work with you. If not, we go back inside and you find your way back to wherever it is you came from."

Keeping his eyes closed, Cendan could only hear her response.

"Really? Keeping your eyes closed? Fine. Whatever. I'll prove it."

He felt a hand squeeze his upper arm and hoped that was Jasmine.

"You can open your eyes now, she's doing something." Jasmine whispered to him. "She's not looking at you, at least."

Cendan cracked his eyes, and through the narrow slit of his vision, he saw that the witch, Heather, had turned her back to him and was holding her fetish – or focus – up in the air with both hands. He still felt an attraction to her, but it was far less now.

"EVA, why didn't you stop her from doing whatever it was she was doing? I could barely think there for a few seconds." Cendan mentally queried.

"*Sorry Cendan, but I couldn't. She was amplifying your already existing attraction to her. That makes it almost impossible for me to stop.*"

Cendan didn't quite understand. "Already existing attraction? I'm not attracted to her!"

EVA gave off what only could be an air of amusement. "*You say not, but even looking at her now, when she's not doing anything, your blood pressure has risen. There's been dilation of blood vessels, and your body temp has risen half a degree.*"

Cendan muttered, "Nonsense," earning himself a quick look from Jasmine.

"What did you say?"

Cendan just tapped the side of his head in response. Jasmine nodded and returned her attention to Heather. Cendan could feel something. It was hard to put into words, however. He could feel the semi familiar twinge, or pull, of the transition when one moves from this world to another. Regardless, if it's the Echo World, or just entering or leaving the Lair. But this was also different; rawer and edgier. He concentrated, and with his new ability to 'see' magic was stunned to see the motion that was normally hidden.

Thousands of the little sparks of magic were swarming past him and Jasmine; maybe millions. They were swirling together in front of Heather, and gathering speed as they went, round and round. He could also see lines of those sparks connecting the witch to the disc being formed before her. It was one of the most stunning displays of light he'd ever seen. No, not light, he corrected himself; magic. Jasmine couldn't see this, at least right now she couldn't.

"Can you feel it Jasmine?" Cendan asked quietly.

Jasmine nodded. "It's strange; it's like when we enter and leave the headquarters, but…"

Cendan nodded. "Yeah, I thought the same thing. I wish you could see this."

Jasmine looked at him strangely. "What do you mean see it? It's right in front of me."

Cendan shook his head. "No, I mean… See the magic. Hold on." Cendan reached out and took Jasmine's shoulder and concentrated.

A gasp escaped Jasmine "What did you do!"

Cendan felt a thrill; he had done it! She was seeing the raw magic. He had done something with magic, on purpose, and it had worked.

"I seem to have shared my vision of magic." Cendan replied. He felt oddly proud of this little victory.

Jasmine didn't say anything, but he could see the look of awe on her face. It was an amazing sight. The sparks slew flew past them, tiny bright sparks of light; blue, green, red, all colors. The disc that was forming was spinning quite fast now and beginning to cave in the middle.

"Your phone!" Cendan whispered to Jasmine. "We didn't set it up!"

Jasmine started and nodded. He felt the contact slip as she quickly ran down the stairs to go back into the headquarters, and to the map room. Cendan half watched her go, but kept an eye on the Bridge that had almost formed. The sparks had tapered off to nothing now; just the disc was there. The edges were starting to take on what for him was the customary circuits and connectors that he always saw on the edges of a Bridge. He was sure the fact that he and the others always saw them differently meant something, but what, he didn't know.

He half wondered what this witch, Heather, saw the Bridges as. Though it really didn't matter; at least as far as he knew. Slowly but surely, the Bridge came into focus, and the long tunnel formed making that connection to the Echo world. Then it was done, Heather lowered her focus, and turned toward him smirking.

"There, happy?"

Cendan nodded. He was impressed though more than a little concerned.

"Where is it going to? Are we going to have anything coming out?"

Heather shook her head. "Shouldn't. I can't make promises, but I opened it up into the Great Desert on the Echo, basically nothing there." Cendan's blank look must have given away his lack of understanding. "You people really know nothing about what you've been fighting? You're this blind? I'm amazed you survived this long."

Heather took her focus and, with her hands, twisted the wood, or at least it looked that way. With a snap, the Bridge closed, and the magic faded away. Cendan could see the ghost of the sparks fade from his vision, and within a minute, all that was left was a slightly thicker area of the always present magic around them.

"I know you've been to the Echo World, Cendan. You, however, only went to the part where the Slyph is the most active. Even in all the years she's had, only a quarter of the place has life in it. The vast majority is a sandy wasteland of nothing. A few odd areas where…" Cendan noted that the witch paused and didn't continue. "It's just empty. No plants; no creatures; nothing."

Jasmine appeared at that moment, a grim expression on her face.

"Nothing. The map was still and quiet. Not a damn thing on it. If I hadn't seen the Bridge forming, I would have not believed it." Mouth set in a hard line Jasmine looked around. "She got rid of the Bridge?"

Cendan nodded. He really hoped that this Heather person had been wrong. This was shaping up to be one hell of a fun day. He'd just wanted to do stuff in the Garden, explore what some of the plants were, what they did, that sort of thing. He refused to believe that they hadn't been planted there for a reason though what it was escaped him for now.

All the journals in the Maker wing were helping of course, but searching paper for things he needed to know was time consuming. The information dump from Oakheart into his focus was far faster, but it was limited to the things Oakheart knew, or could remember at the time he put it all in there. Which, after a thousand plus years of being the Slyph's plaything, wasn't a very complete picture. Some of it was clear and precise, like anything dealing with EVA. Other parts were pretty weak, or even nonexistent. It was frustrating; he had been so sure at first that the key would hold everything he needed.

And now this: the map apparently broken, most likely in the attack that killed Sal; and a witch, an outsider who could work magic, giving information and offering to help. And Marcus seemed to be getting more bitter and angry by the day and placing all that anger and bitterness on Cendan. Add in the information about Grellnot, and the warning from the Elf King that his twice damned bargain was remembered, and Cendan was not having the best day.

Chapter 4

"Well, do we have her look at it?" Cendan asked Jasmine. "It's going to be your call, Jasmine. Marcus will lose it either way, but it might be better if it didn't come from me." Pausing for a moment, Cendan let out a long breath. "Marcus is getting a bit dark as of late."

Jasmine didn't answer at first, her eyes locked onto the witch who was tapping her focus against her leg with a decidedly annoyed expression on her face.

"He's just a worrier, Cendan. Marcus is a good guy. As for the witch, I really don't know. Can't you figure it out? I mean, it's a Maker thing right? You're a Maker."

Cendan's shoulders fell a bit. "Yeah, but I have no idea how long it might take me to figure it out. Remember, most of the journals in that room are old, really old. And half the time they don't make a hell of a lot of sense until you read something else in some other journal. I think most of the authors sort of expected whoever picked them up to have a solid firm grounding in being a Maker already. Not someone like me, with a highly incomplete picture of all of it.

So yeah, could I fix it without her? Maybe, given enough time. But do we have the time? If Bridges are being formed, and we don't have a clue where or when, and there's a war going on between Grellnot and the Slyph, can we afford to wait for me to figure it out?" Cendan hated feeling this way, frustrated and unsure.

"I know. That's the only reason I'm even considering this," Jasmine answered. "I just... Everything I was ever taught, everything I ever even heard about people like her – those who deal with the echo world, outside of us, outside of the Bridgefinders – screams not to trust her. But we are flying blind here. What's worth more, the legacy of what I was taught, or figuring out what happened to the map?" Jasmine leaned against the wall, her eyes fixed on Heather, who smirked back.

"She knows it too Cendan. She knows that for all basic purposes, she has me, us, in a hard place. Marcus would scream at me to get rid of her and never even think about it again. You are on the other end, I think. Correct me if I'm wrong, but I think you lean towards letting her in. And I'm stuck in the damn middle." Jasmine glanced at her watch. "Getting late. Marcus will be done brooding soon. He usually eats in the next hour, creature of habit that man. If we are going to do this, let's do this now."

Cendan was somewhat surprised. "Really? You're going to let her look at the map?" He had wanted her to, if only so he could watch this witch do her thing, and try to learn from it. He already had some ideas on things after watching her form a Bridge. He figured, though, that Jasmine, though more reasonable than Marcus had ever been, wouldn't go against her background, her training.

Jasmine slow nodded. "Yes, though I may regret the hell out of this. Let's tell her, get this done, and get her out. If all goes well, Marcus may not even know. He can only tell where we are in the headquarters, and that's only if he's looking for us. Pray he doesn't start to look."

Jasmine stood and gestured to Heather, who for once looked somewhat surprised. As she came over to Cendan and Jasmine, however, her seemingly normal expression of slight condescension returned.

"So, I take it you Finders came to your senses and are going to let me help?" Heather asked as she joined them at the head of the stairs.

Jasmine said nothing, but rolled her eyes in response.

"Yeah, but this is a quick thing. In, you do what you can to check the map, and then out. There's someone we'd like to avoid." Cendan paused, then continued, "He doesn't like... your kind."

Heather laughed, a rather melodic one Cendan thought, then caught himself. Another glamour? A trick to attract his attention? EVA hadn't said anything, but then again, EVA hadn't said much about any of this, unless he asked her directly. He reached out with his new sight, but didn't see anything disturbing the flow of magic around her. Maybe she just had a really nice laugh.

"That would be Marcus. Yes, I know who he is. You didn't think I came here without doing my homework, did you? I know all about all of you, or at least as much as I could find out. Marcus's feelings about my kind are very well known. Even without talking to any resources on the Echo World. We, who are outside your little club, do talk to each other." Heather grinned at them both. "Well come on, I'm actually interested to see this place I've heard about."

Jasmine motioned Heather towards the stairs, leading the way herself. Cendan followed behind them both. This way, at least the witch couldn't make a break for it once they were inside; at least not without having to go through one or both of them. Cendan knew that it might not be much of a deterrent, but it was the best they had. And if Marcus did show up, one of them might be able to run enough interference to not have him figure things out. Mentally, he wasn't liking the branches that this choice gave him – way too many ended up with bad things happening – but none of the choices were very good.

They stood in front of the barrier, the wall that required them to use their foci to open. Heather said nothing until Jasmine raised her focus and the wall melted away. Air escaped the witch then, a soft gasp of surprise. Jasmine stepped through the opening, followed by Heather, and then Cendan. As soon as they were in the hallway of the lair, Heather leaned forward and caught her breath.

"That was impressive. And more than a little surprising." Head raised, the witch took in her surroundings. "This place, it's not on earth, is it? I can tell; the flow here, the magic, it's stronger. Different, but stronger."

Cendan nodded, somewhat surprised that she could figure that out so fast. Magic to her, though, was second nature. She knew it.

"Yes, based on what we know, it was built on what amounts to a huge chunk of rock somehow in between our world and the Echo world."

Heather closed her eyes, and just as quickly opened them again. "You mean the Slyph's world. Yes, I can feel it."

A sharp gesture by Jasmine ended their conversation as they followed her in silence. Cendan watched Heather as she took the place in; the various light sources, the many and varied doors, all of it. The whole time she nodded with a small smile on her face, which he hoped was a sign of some actual approval. Finally, two long hallways later, Jasmine pointed to the door that led to the map.

"Let me go in first, just in case." Jasmine whispered as she straightened her jacket and stepped into the map room. "All clear."

Jasmine's voice drifted out to them in the hall. Breath escaped Cendan in a long exhale. He hadn't even been aware he was holding it. Heather followed Jasmine, with Cendan right behind.

"Here's the map. Do what you need to do, but be fast." Cendan pointed to the huge wooden map taking up one wall. He still couldn't get too close to the thing; there was still that resistance to him. It was like magnets sliding apart. He could force contact, but it didn't like it. Must be a Maker thing, he thought, making a mental note to look it up.

Heather's face lit up at the sight of the thing. "You all may be a bunch of ignorant idiots, but man, you come from some insanely talented and powerful magic users. This thing is incredible!"

"EVA, can you tell if Marcus is heading this way?" Cendan queried EVA. She'd been oddly silent since the earlier interactions with Heather, and this was a way to test it.

"*Yes... I think.*" EVA's voice sounded distant and had a distinct tinny sound which was odd for her.

"Everything ok? You sound odd to me." Cendan still wasn't used to this mental communication.

"*Yes... but, there seems to be some odd interference with our link. I'm checking it out.*" And with that, EVA's presence in his mind faded into the background.

"I have EVA monitoring Marcus, or at least trying to. But let's be fast in here." Cendan waved Heather forward. "Go ahead." He, however, paused and focused on her with his new ability. If nothing else, at least it was seeing how magic came together and worked. His new vision unfolded in his mind, and he could take in the view. As usual, here in the lair, the normal bright dots on magic from his world were mixed with the threads of magic that seemed to be the way it worked in the Slyph's world.

He had wondered about that often: why it looked different. The only theory that made any sense to him was that magic was thicker, stronger on the Slyph's world. More creatures used it, and it seemed to him to be more powerful. The magic of his world was not as strong, but there were a lot less using it at any one time, therefore one could draw on more of it, given enough time.

Here in the map room, outside the map itself, the mix was pretty even: threads and shining dots, hundreds of colors, shining bright. But the map - the map was a wonder. Large solid bands of threads mixed with large solid clumps of shining stars. Touching, and somehow working together, but not fully intergrated. Heather raised one hand, clutching her focus – no fetish, he reminded himself. Whatever it was called, she used it like a focus, centering her power in the middle of it this time.

Threads spun toward the circle, forming a web projecting out of it, a long series of the shining dots of the human world's magic flew down the center of this web, but oddly for once, they were all the same color; blue. Only blue. Cendan wasn't sure what that meant exactly. He'd have to find a way to ask Heather without getting a sarcastic response. This mix, the web and the line of blue sparks, flowed over the map, the sparks searching the map like some sort of starry probe – or at least that was the only way he could seem to picture it. The web held the map in place as if it was going to try to get away.

There! Near the bottom, there was a small motion in a mass of solid threads! Cendan watched as the probing sparks flew toward that spot. The surface of the map in that area writhed in sudden motion, and he could hear Jasmine, startled by it, take a step back. Hairs on the back of his neck stood up as he took several steps back as-well. What exactly was going on, he wasn't sure, but it couldn't be good.

With a crack, the wood in that area split and out came something from an entomologist's nightmare. Cendan, horrified a bit, felt himself shudder. He hated bugs. He knew it was irrational, but the feeling had only gotten worse since the day he went through the portal. Those Klacker things had creeped him out, and this thing was just as bad, if on a smaller scale. Grub-like with wings, a round snapping mouth, and tentacles instead of legs, the thing flew into the air, its two sets of wings making a whine in the air that set Cendan's teeth on edge.

"What the hell is that?" Cendan felt himself shudder. He could see the web though the one that Heather had created was keeping it back, as the thing lunged forward in the air, sliding back from the barrier. Jasmine had grabbed a small can of pepper spray from her key chain and kept her eye on the thing as it flew in fast short bursts.

Heather didn't say anything at first, but her shoulders tensed up. Her voice came then, tight and clipped.

"We have to kill it. Now. Fast."

Cendan looked around, unsure of what to use, there wasn't much here other than the map. Thankfully Jasmine stepped forward and, holding the spray ready, glanced at Cendan.

"If she can hold it, I'll spray it with this stuff. Dunno if it will kill it, but it hopefully won't like it." It was hard to hear her over the whine the thing was making, but Cendan got the gist.

Cendan looked around, still trying to find something to whack the thing with, when he had an idea. The lights! They looked like torches, maybe they could be taken down, hit the thing with one? He'd never actually tried to remove one of the lights, but it was worth a shot, he told himself.

"EVA? Any help?"

But oddly, EVA was silent still. Her presence was there, but still muffled; quiet. Rushing over to a light, he was relived to find that, yes, it did come out pretty easily. The one in his hand had six glowing balls that blinked, like eyes.

Sort of like spider eyes, the thought came, which was creepy enough based on the situation at hand.

"Ok, spray it!" Cendan yelled.

Jasmine let loose as Heather clamped the net down on the flying grub, and two things happened at once. As soon as the pepper spray hit the thing, a screech tore through the air, reverberating through the room. The thing also, however, fell to the ground allowing Cendan to, with an overhand two handed smash, crush the thing.

Chapter 5

Silence fell. Heather, Jasmine, and Cendan all exchanged glances at each other, and the nearly foot-long flying thing lying on the floor.

"Marcus had to have heard that." Jasmine was the first to break the silence. "I'll get Heather outside. Make something up to tell him until we can figure this out." Grabbing Heather by the arm, despite the start of protests, Jasmine quickly ran out of the room towards the exit.

"What was that!?" Marcus came barreling into the room, focus held up. Cendan could only wonder at what he thought of the scene in front of him. A dead flying grub of large size; the smell of pepper spray in the air; and Cendan holding a wall-light like a two handed club with bits of... whatever the thing was still sticking to the glass on the light.

Eyes narrowed, Marcus lowered his hand slowly. "Ok, talk."

Cendan sighed. Jasmine should have stayed and talked to Marcus, not him. Got to think fast, he told himself.

"Well... Jasmine and I were talking about the map, about how we hadn't seen any Bridges since that day, right? I was talking to EVA and realized her and the map were linked somehow. We came in here, and while we were seeing if EVA could find anything wrong with the map, that thing," Cendan paused and pointed at the remains of the creature on the floor. "That thing came out of the map. You can see the crack it made. Jasmine had the forethought to spray the thing with pepper spray, and I whacked it." Cendan held up the wall torch.

"Marcus, I think the map is broken. I think that it's been broken since that day." Cendan wasn't looking at Marcus. His eyes were glued to the map in front of him. "I don't know how to fix this yet…"

The blow came fast, hard. Cendan went down involuntarily, grabbing the side of his head as pain exploded.

"You broke the map! It was fine," Marcus yelled, standing over Cendan, rage writ across his face. Cendan was stunned. Through the pain, he fumbled to think to something; anything to say. Instead, Marcus continued.

"You and that damn machine broke it!" Marcus slammed his fist into the map, his focus, the ring digging into the wood. "I used to dream about that thing coming back online. I used to wish for it, and now, like everything with you, you've ruined it."

Cendan slowly came to his feet. He could feel a small drip of liquid on the side of his face; blood? Maybe from the ring.

"Marcus, calm the hell down. That thing broke the damn map. Not me; not EVA; that!" Cendan pointed to the remains on the floor. "It probably got there the day the Slyph attacked and Sal died! Think for a damn second, Marcus!" Cendan watched Marcus carefully. He wasn't sure what had triggered this rage, this level of anger, but he wasn't about to get sucker punched in the head again. Marcus he knew would be angry about the witch, but violence?

Marcus's face, tightened, his lips a thin line on an already drawn and sharp face.

"Don't you talk about the Bridgefinder that you got killed. For the last two weeks I've sat and thought, each day realizing more and more that you, Cendan, you are the cause of all of this ... this falling apart of the Bridgefinders."

"Sal's death; the map; the breaking of traditions; the tainting of Jasmine; all of it. It's your fault. We should have let Grellnot damn well have you. I wish I could go back in time and take that focus of yours that day when you dropped it, the first night we all met. Take it and send you away. That would have been better than this!" Marcus held up his fist, white knuckled and pale. "I have been a Bridgefinder all my life. My parents were, and their parents before them. I honor this with my very life!"

"You, Cendan Key, you mock it. And now, your stupidity and carelessness have broken the very tool we need to keep this world safe." Marcus spat on the floor. "That thing I'm sure was something you brought back from your little trip to the Slyph's world."

Cendan reached out to EVA mentally, but once again found her hard to reach. Prioritize! He told himself. Cendan opened his mouth to respond to Marcus, but closed it again.

Jasmine saved the day as she walked into the map room and stopped short.

"What is going on?" Jasmine rushed to Cendan, checking the mark on his face. "What happened?"

Not taking his eyes off Marcus, Cendan let out a slow breath. "Marcus here blames me for the map, sucker punched me in the head. Apparently I'm the worst thing that ever happened to this place."

Jasmine turned to Marcus, eyes wide. "Marcus?"

Marcus pointed at Cendan. "I want him gone, Jasmine. Don't you get it? Everything we've done, everything we've worked for, our parents worked for, everything the Bridgefinders is under threat because of him!" Marcus turned to walk away, but instead stopped and stared Jasmine down. "Where were you just now Jasmine? I know you were here.."

Jasmine grabbed Cendan's arm. "Marcus, you're being ridiculous. Cendan is—"

Marcus cut her off. "Gone Jasmine. I don't care about anything. You're staying, he's going. Forever."

Jasmine stood up straight. "Hell no. What is in your head? Cendan is a Maker, remember? You want to send away the only Maker we've had in over a thousand years?"

Marcus barked a short laugh. "Maker? He's only making a mockery of us. Of all of us. Don't you see it, Jasmine? In the short time he's been here; this talk of magic; breaking things; getting Sal killed. He's the cause of all the pain we've had."

Jasmine and Cendan exchanged glances. Marcus didn't know about Heather at least. Whatever was going on with him that knowledge would probably push him even farther down this dark path he was on.

"Cendan isn't going anywhere, Marcus." Jasmine answered quietly. "I don't know where you are coming from, you're one of my oldest friends, and I've been proud to call you such, but this… this is insanity."

Marcus grimaced in response. "Jasmine, I know you and he once dated, but get away from him. Just... stay here, and he leaves."

Jasmine looked at Marcus and blanched. She turned to Cendan and whispered. "I think Marcus is... jealous."

Cendan however was being pulled in a thousand different directions. Anger; that buried deep emotion threatened to come out and escalate quickly with Marcus. Confusion over what was going on and why; worry over what had happened to Marcus in the last two weeks as he had sat in the barrier room stewing over the changes that had happened.

Slowly, Jasmine's whisper made its way through the crowd of thoughts in his head. "Jealous? What?" was all he could mumble in return. His head hurt. "Jealous as in… of you."

"Look, let me walk you out of this room. He won't do anything with me here, at least I damn well hope not." Jasmine locked eyes with Cendan, making sure he understood. Glancing at Marcus, who still wound tight was standing with his arms crossed, watching them whisper to each other.

Without saying anything else, Jasmine led Cendan out of the map room and down the hall, out of earshot of Marcus. "How are you?" Jasmine asked as she took another look at the wound.

"Damn it hurts. The cut hurts, my skull hurts. What do you mean jealous?" he said, wincing as he gently touched the sore spot from the blow.

"It's no excuse, I find this all really hard to believe honestly, but Marcus is jealous of you. You're the Maker; you saved us; you went to the echo world; and you found Oakheart. All of it." Jasmine sighed. "And you dated me."

Cendan lowered his hand from his head. "What does that have to do with anything?"

"Marcus and I are Bridgefinder kids. Our parents were Bridgefinders, and on and on. Marcus has long had a level of interest in me that I don't share. He knows I don't. And in the abstract, he was ok with it. He didn't like it, but it was ok. But now, you, the person who did all these things that he the leader of what's left of the Bridgefinders couldn't even come close to doing, that person also used to date me? Bitter pill for him." Jasmine sighed. "I never thought he would do this, however. I thought we were giving him space to get through things with Sal's death. We should have not let him stew."

Cendan gingerly nodded. "You think his jealousy and anger have pushed him to, well what, hating me?"

Jasmine slumped back against the wall. "I don't know, maybe. But I'm at a loss what to do about it."

Cendan was dumbfounded. He knew Marcus was unhappy, that much had been made clear before, but this attack, the sheer bitterness of it all. It baffled him. And now Marcus wanted him out of the Bridgefinders. Cendan wasn't sure he could even do that. He hadn't really paid much attention to what Marcus being the head of the group really meant.

"Maybe… maybe I should take a few days, let Marcus calm down some." Cendan said trying to find the right path, the right set of branches.

"This is crazy, Cendan. The map is broken; EVA can't find the Bridges to keep them under control without it. Only a Maker can fix the map, and you're the only one we have. And now Marcus wants you gone? Right now? When you're the only thing that can fix it? He doesn't even know about the Grellnot-Slyph fight yet!" Jasmine slid down the wall to sit on the floor. "I wish Sal was here. He seemed to be able to always find the right tone to get Marcus to listen, without setting him off."

Neither of them said anything for a while, each lost in their thoughts. Jasmine, trying to figure out how everything had gone so badly, and Cendan wondering what to do and where to go. On top of it all, the issues with communication with EVA were odd as well. He still didn't know enough about EVA to venture a guess as to what was going on with her. Jasmine gave out a long sigh, breaking the silence.

"Ok, we have to do something. So here's my thoughts. You go get a few things together, do what you need to do, and head out for a few days. Go back to your house, take your focus with you, just in case. Give me a few days to try to get Marcus to change his mind. Or at least to figure out where all this came from. Not sure I feel particularly safe here either now, truthfully."

EVA. Why couldn't he talk to her? Was it something with that witch woman, Heather? Some part of the map issue? Marcus, who only a few short weeks ago had celebrated the return of EVA, now blamed her for the map breaking. For a second he wondered if Marcus had anything to do with the recent issues, but discarded the idea. Even as angry as he was with the man, Marcus wouldn't do anything like that; at least he believed he wouldn't.

Cendan nodded. "Maybe come with me? Leave him here to think things through, then come back to talk to him? I don't want him attacking you or anything."

Jasmine snorted. "Marcus wouldn't do that."

One finger extended to the drying cut on his face as he said, "I never thought he'd do this either, but it's there. Whatever story he's invented in his head, it's not one that says anything good about me, and possibly you."

Jasmine started to answer, but held back for a few before finally talking. "That's true, but I think I can do better here. If things look bad, or I can't make any headway, I'll come to your place as quickly as I can."

Cendan didn't like it, at all. He couldn't force Jasmine to come with him, and their options were highly limited in terms of who could talk to Marcus. It didn't seem to him that Marcus had any friends, really; the Bridgefinders were his life. That was it. Cendan realized, however, that he wasn't much better. He hadn't talked to, nor even thought about, the people he knew before all this started what, a month ago? Month and a half?

He was a very different person now, in some ways, but not in others. He still found people difficult to understand, or even deal with in some ways. Marcus's newly found rage, however, shook him a bit. Not because it was aimed at him though that wasn't a pleasant thing. It was because that branch was one he could have gone down in the right circumstances, and he damn well didn't like that. Jasmine was right though; go back to his old house, get a few days separation, and hopefully all this Marcus stuff gets fixed, then they could fix the real problem. The Map and the war on the Echo World. All of the actual 'threaten the world' stuff.

"Ok, Jasmine. I don't like it, but I can't think of a better path."

Cendan wanted to get a few things from his room here, grab a journal or two from the Maker wing, and touch base with EVA, if possible. He wasn't sure how communication would go with EVA; he could still feel her in his head, but still muffled. Maybe being in the actual room would clear it up.

Jasmine nodded. "I'll be careful, Cendan. I'll give him some time to cool down and then talk to him. We can get this behind us and move on."

The smile she flashed didn't show much promise of that, however.

Chapter 6

Grellnot wiped its face again on its dirty sleeve and arm. Goblins, especially fat ones were rather greasy eating, and it didn't want to get its shiny treasures too dirty with goblin blood and fat. It had followed the tribe it had ambushed before and hunted down a particularly fat one for a meal. Grellnot, however, had some thinking he needed to do.

The Slyph was going to come for it. Grellnot knew this. It may not be the smartest creature the Slyph had ever created, but it was cunning, and knew strategy. Right now she was powerful, but only the power of this world, her world. More dangerous to Grellnot was her army of creatures. Those creatures, or at least most of them, thought of the Slyph as a living god. A god that gave them life.

Picking its teeth with a cracked goblin finger-bone, Grellnot smiled. If the Slyph was the god who gave them life, Grellnot was the god who brought them death. Pausing, Grellnot stood up a bit straighter. Maybe... maybe Grellnot could use that. The Slyph's army of creatures were just too many for Grellnot to stop on its own. But if Grellnot had its own creatures, maybe Grellnot could stop enough for Grellnot to get to the Slyph?

"Grellnot can't make creatures, not like her. But maybe Grellnot can make creatures follow Grellnot. They not love Grellnot, no one loves Grellnot."

A low whine came from Grellnot, and it rocked back and forth on its heels. "Grellnot not loved, not liked. But Grellnot is feared. All creatures know what happens if Grellnot catches you." The goblin finger bone flew through the air as Grellnot spat it out. "Grellnot needs an army of its own. An army to fight for Grellnot, to kill for Grellnot!"

Grellnot stood and sniffed the air, reaching out in all directions with every sense it had, including its new ability to sense and see magic. The goblins were nearby of course, but goblins were small things, cowardly, not strong. Ok eating though, and enough of them might help.

"Grellnot needs strong things, mighty things. Giants, Jabbers, and more."

Grellnot sensed a village of dwarves a few miles away underground, but they wouldn't be much help. Dwarves didn't love the Slyph either, but they hated Grellnot. Tasted like dirt and dust, dwarves did; not tasty at all. Finally, a wisp of a scent, a village of Jabbers, far, but no place was really far for Grellnot anymore. A huge leap and Grellnot vanished, leaving only the slight remains of the fat goblin it had been eating, and a feeling of rot and decay behind.

The Slyph was both pleased and annoyed. The creature she had created for the single job of breaking the Bridgefinders map had succeeded. Without that map, the Finders were nearly blind. Even better, this seemed to mean that the machine, the fake mind the Makers had made, had lost a great deal of its power with the destruction of the map.

"I should have destroyed the map instead of the machine when I had the chance before." The Slyph spoke out loud to her hounds, her now constant companions.

Her little creation was dead now, sadly; that was annoying. Even more annoying was that the death was due to the interference of a human outside the Bridgefinders. She wasn't sure why or how, but she knew magic had been worked on one of her creatures; magic that the Bridgefinders didn't use. It must have been one of the humans that interacted with her world and her creatures. She knew all about those types. She'd been happy to work with them once, but they were still so limited, so slow.

Worse, they didn't bow to her easily. They summoned her creatures, her creations to make them do work for them! Humans, if they were allowed to live at all, should serve her and her children, not the other way around. But yet, one of those humans, one of the kind called a wizard, now a witch – that's right, a witch – had helped the Bridgefinders. Witch. Humans were so limited in their understandings: witch, wizard -it didn't matter. Both worked the same power, but because one was normally female and one male, they had different names. Like that mattered at all to the magic.

It had been useful, the divisions between humans. So tribal; easy hate. But if things were changing, if those humans outside the Bridgefinders who could work power, true power, joined the Finders, she had problems. Problems. The very idea that she, the Slyph, could have problems was laughable, or would have been a short time ago. Now, she faced a human world where a Maker had come forth, and a rebellion in the form of Grellnot on her own.

Grellnot. Where was the wretched thing? She couldn't track it, at least not directly. If a creature had seen it she would know, but only if she went looking for it. And looking took time, far too much time. However, as much of a problem as Grellnot was, she did have the upper hand. Grellnot was singular, alone, unloved and hated. Feared. She had an army, thousands of creatures that loved her as a living goddess. She just couldn't let Grellnot get near her that was all.

The Slyph wasn't sure if Grellnot could feast upon her or not, truthfully, but he'd try, and being taste tested wasn't in the list of things she wanted to do. Her hounds would offer some protection if it came to that. Grellnot had to make the first move, she wasn't going to chase it around, not while she had a bit of an opening on the human's world.

"Grellnot will come to me, and I will end its miserable life. It may even thank me for it before it dies." The Slyph spoke to a hound as it rested its head on her hand. "Don't worry, I won't make you eat the foul thing."

The Hound shuddered at this information, its tail whipping back and forth.

"Come, I have to make sure when our former servant, Grellnot, finally attacks, that it won't last long."

Cendan found himself standing at the exit to the HQ. He wasn't sure how things had gotten so bad with Marcus so fast. It had been obvious that Marcus, and he weren't going to be friends from somewhat early on. But this; this had been way outside what Cendan had expected. His bag was heavy in his hand; clothes, books, and a few other things stuffed inside it. A month or so ago he'd have been pretty happy to have Marcus kick him out to his old house, to walk away. That did seem like a lifetime ago, so much had happened to him since.

Traveling to the Echo World; meeting Oakheart; his troubling deal with the Elves; talking Grellnot out of killing him; the resurrection of EVA; the death of Sal. EVA. His visit to her place in the lair had been far from helpful. Her voice was still muted, even there. Worse, he could tell she was trying to talk to him, or at least he got that feeling. But something was stopping her, holding her back. It was frustrating. Marcus wouldn't even let him tell him about it either. He hated to leave her as well. Marcus and Jasmine didn't have a clue what to do with EVA, not even how to fix her if something went wrong.

For that matter, he was still tweaking everything to make it work better. The job to get EVA back 'alive' during the attack by the Slyph had been a rush job, and not the way Cendan had wanted it to be long term. Maybe that was the issue with her; something he and Sal had fixed in a rush had partially given way again. Marcus, however, wasn't going to give him the time to even try to figure it out, and he didn't have much time left.

He'd grabbed a few books from the Maker Wing that he thought might be somewhat useful at least. One on the creation of foci, another that appeared to be the notes of the Maker before Oakheart. It was odd, but there always seemed to be only one Maker at a time. Until the break with Oakheart, they followed each other like clockwork. But then again, Oakheart hadn't died; he'd been stuck in a tree, used as a conduit for Earth's magic for the Slyph to use.

At least he still had his focus on him. He'd had it when they had worked on the map, and Marcus hadn't included it in his rant to kick him out. Cendan had little doubt that if Marcus knew he had it on him, the demand for its return would be swift. Fishing the Key out, its touch and warmth comforted him. It was as much a part of him as the hand he held it in. It was also loaded with raw knowledge from Oakheart, most of which he still couldn't make sense of.

Cendan still believed that the main reason for that was that Oakheart himself didn't know what he still knew or didn't know. Fifteen hundred years kept in the form of a tree would, and could, make you forget things, even important things. He'd be mentally searching for information on, say, Bridges and why they looked different to each person. He'd get a blast of information but it would have gaps, places where there was, nothing. 'Mental whiteout' Cendan muttered to himself.

Clearing his mind of his musings, Cendan held up the focus and opened the portal to leave. The translation felt odd this time to him, however; as if the connection was wobbling. Just as quickly as it came, the translation was done, and he was once again at the bottom of the basement steps of the Red Orchid.

Two things struck him at once: first off, it was later than he thought it was – the sky was starting to darken. And secondly, standing at the top of the steps was the witch, Heather.

"Finally! That Jasmine woman told me to leave and wait here. I've been sitting here for nearly two hours!" Heather hid none of her irritation. It was only then her eyes lighted upon the bag he was holding and the cut on his face. "So what happened?" was her only question, her tone considerably calmer.

"Marcus happened," Cendan answered. "He wasn't happy about doing anything with the map. He blamed me for it, and in his anger, sucker punched me in the head and kicked me out."

Heather gave off a low whistle. "Sounds like your friend Marcus there has some anger issues."

Cendan climbed the stairs, standing in rapidly vanishing light.

"Marcus is not my friend." Cendan dropped the bag with a thud on the ground.

"What? But aren't you like a, what's that word you all use, a Maker?" Heather asked confused. "We don't call them that, but for you all isn't that a big deal?"

It was Cendan's turn to be surprised, then; what did she mean? There were Makers outside of the Bridgefinders? As soon as the thought came to him, he was slightly embarrassed he had never even considered the possibility. He'd taken Marcus and Jasmine at their word that there was nothing but bad about those who were outside the Bridgefinders.

"Ah well... yes. But Marcus blames me for, well, everything apparently. Jasmine thinks it's just a case of hurt pride, but hurt pride doesn't go around hitting people and kicking them out."

Heather nodded slowly. "You'd be surprised. Pride has made people do many a stupid thing in the world, Cendan."

Cendan nodded, but wanted to get back to the subject she had casually mentioned; about other Makers, or whatever they called them, since they don't call them that, whoever they are.

"Uh, Heather, what you just said, what do you mean? Makers, or whatever you call them, or us, or... whatever. I guess I'm confused."

Laughter greeted his question, and to his surprise he found himself smiling at the sound of it. Immediately, he suspected some sort of compulsion was being used, but when he summoned his magic sight, there was nothing active. Chalking it up to just stress relief, Cendan focused his attention on Heather. Tossing her hair back, Heather grinned at Cendan; that same smart-aleck look that seemed to be her normal face.

"I forget how little you guys know. I find it funny really. All I heard growing in my powers and abilities is about how the mighty Bridgefinders hate us, and we can never let them know anything about how we operate. And now, after seeing the Bridgefinders up close, I see a dying group of people, in denial of their true powers, clinging to the remnants of what must have been an incredible past."

Cendan grimaced, but it wasn't something he hadn't thought of. Oakheart had told him that this wasn't the way it was supposed to be, this denial of magic. How had the Bridgefinders come to this, a whimpering end? Shaking himself, he turned his thoughts to the now. The past would be something he'd have to look into, if he ever had the time.

"Yes well, educate me then," Cendan responded. "Look, Heather, your help in there was more than valuable. We'd never have even driven that thing out of the map if you hadn't been there. Just tell me, ok?"

For once Heather didn't respond immediately. "I'd like to Cendan, but I don't think it's a good idea; at least, not without talking to people. You have to understand, the separation between the Bridgefinders and the rest of us is old; really old. I'm not saying there's prejudice or anything, but there may be people who really don't want you and yours to know about us."

"That would make sense if I was still a Bridgefinder, but I got kicked out, remember?" he answered pointing to the bag on the ground. "At this point I don't think I'm a Bridgefinder."

Silence fell over them, Cendan watching Heather, and Heather looking Cendan.

"Ok, I'll do this. You give me a ride to… a place. I'll ask them what they want to do."

Cendan nodded. "That's fair."

He wanted to know a lot more, like who was she going to ask? He'd never really thought that the others, the ones that were labeled witches and wizards, warlocks and sorcerers, or whatever else they could be called, had any organization. He just figured each was a solo agent able to do whatever they wanted. Mentally he chalked that up to a lack of understanding, something he didn't like. It betrayed a prejudice, an assumption that whoever he was involved with was the right answer, the only answer.

Chapter 7

Mentally, he returned to his old standby; the branches. In his mind, he could see the choices and where they may lead him. Some he discarded because the choice had already been made for him; Marcus had kicked him out, so he didn't have choices involving the Bridgefinders at the moment. Another choice was to end this and go home, wait it out. But the branches there were decidedly not pleasant. Assuming it was true, that Grellnot, and the Slyph were at war, not having him as a Bridgefinder meant bad things, for both him and Jasmine. Even to Marcus, he grudgingly admitted to himself. Going with Heather led to some branches that at least seemed to offer some decent outcomes.

"What magic are you working?" Heather asked him curiously, breaking his concentration.

"What?" Cendan asked, bringing his attention back to her.

"Magic; you were working it right then. The sparks of it where flying around you in a very unusual way. I've never seen that, and I've seen a lot of magic get worked." Her eyes appraised him, and for once he didn't detect any mocking in them.

"I wasn't working magic.; just a mental exercise I do to see where choices could lead…"

Heather held up a finger. "Scrying. You were scrying. Never seen a scryer spell like that one though. Interesting."

Cendan laughed. "It wasn't a spell I was just making a decision."

Heather didn't respond, instead just cocking her eyebrow in a 'whatever you say' manner. Cendan found himself instantly wondering what she had seen. It was just his mental exercise, he'd done it many a time, going back years. It wasn't magic, was it? For some reason, he found the idea rather unsettling. If he had actually been doing some sort of magic for years and not known that, he didn't like. He'd chalked up that little exercise to logic and weighing of factors. It had been a mental thing. But perhaps it had been magic all along, a scrying of some kind that meant the answers weren't based on logic and fact, but some ethereal force that he had very little understanding of?

He had prided himself on that; making decisions on logic and understanding. If Heather was right…

"Are we going to go soon? It's getting dark." Heather asked breaking into his head full of new self-doubt.

"Yeah… I guess. I uh, well my car isn't here, it's at my old house. Dunno if I should borrow one of the Bridgefinder cars or not."

A petulant eye-roll greeted this piece of information.

"Ok fine, we will get a cab to your house then." Heather snapped at him. "I just want to get moving, I've waited around long enough."

Cendan grabbed his bag and gestured her to take the lead. Truthfully, his mind was trying to make sense again of everything. A month ago he felt like a curtain had been ripped from a window that he didn't know existed, showing him the world of the Bridgefinders. A world of magic, creatures, violence and danger. Now things are torn, but even more. Kicked out of his new home, new knowledge of the users of magic outside the Bridgefinders, and the idea that he'd been using magic for years, and not known it.

Add in getting punched – punched! – by Marcus, and quite simply this day could end anytime now and he didn't think he'd have ever been so happy to have it do so. Heather quickly called a cab, Cendan noted with some level of wry amusement. Giving the driver his address, Cendan sat in silence, staring out the window as the outside world flew past. He loved this town at night, he realized; not that he often saw it that way. It seemed that after night fell, he'd be inside, away from it all. There was something rather pretty about it though, just different enough to get his attention away from this gnawing self-doubt that had engulfed him with Heather's spell casting question.

They rode on in silence, but shortly they pulled in front of his old house. It looked odd to him now, even stranger than it had the last time he'd been here. The lawn service had done its job; the place had been mowed. All the bills were on autopay so Cendan didn't have to worry about them, at least for now. Quickly paying the driver, they stood in the gathering gloom for a moment before Heather broke the silence.

"Nice place. Must have some money to live around here." She glanced around his old neighborhood.

"Yeah well, before... Well before all this, I was pretty successful in business." He really didn't want to go into what he had done for a living. That would just drive more questions and thoughts he wasn't quite ready to deal with yet. "C'mon, let's go in. I'll get my car keys and we can head out. And mail, I probably better clean up the mail."

Cendan unlocked his front door to find a small pile of the stuff. His old place had one of those in the door mail slots, handy, but capable of quite a mess if not dealt with.

Most of it, of course, was junk mail, a few letters from old clients probably wanting to know where he was. He'd gone dark on his old job of consulting when he'd moved into the Bridgefinders lair. There wasn't much reason to do it in a place where modern technology didn't really work for the most part. Dropping his bag on the floor, he quickly sorted through the small pile.

"Nice place inside as well." Heather remarked as she looked around. "It's very you."

"What do you mean?" he asked as he flipped through a bunch of sales flyers; how many new cars did they think he needed?

"It's nice, but clean, organized, and a bit… sterile." Heather shot back, with a slightly amused tone. He raised his eyes at that to see her face bearing that slightly mocking grin again.

"Sterile?" he asked, not sure if he really wanted to know what she meant. He just liked things his way. Simple.

"Yeah, Sterile." Heather didn't provide any details, Cendan was happy to hear.

Finally, he parred the mail down to fifteen letters that he figured at some point soon he better talk to. He'd have to get back into all this now that he apparently was going to have to go back to his old life. Darkness was falling fast outside, and he had told Heather he'd get her to wherever it was they needed to go. He did wonder why they hadn't just taken a cab to where it was, instead of coming here first. Heather had wanted to come here though. Why?

"Well let me get my keys and we can be off." Cendan headed toward the office where he kept the keys, noting that the cleaning crew had come as well; no dust to speak of.

"Actually, let's just stay here tonight, and leave in the morning. It's dark now, and it might be better to talk to people in the light." Heather sat on the couch with a slightly expectant look.

"Uh ... excuse me?" was all Cendan could think to say. What was the game here?

"Don't worry, I'll throw some wards on the house for the night, make sure nothing attacks or messes with you or I." She replied as she pulled her fetish off her wrist where she wore it. "Won't take a minute. Just need to step outside."

Cendan watched her walk outside before he started and ran after her.

"Hey now, my neighbors..." He stopped once he saw her. Heather was standing in front of his house, facing away from it, her red and blue hair barely visible in the fading light. What truly stopped him, though, was the feeling he got, his skin pricked as if something had rubbed it with steel wool that had been frozen. Wards, he thought. Protections. I need to see this.

Opening himself to the sight, he saw what she was working. A series of layers of magic, sparks pushed together tightly, forming an invisible to the normal eye. Green, then red, then blue layers formed around the place. Above and below, he could somehow see the walls in the ground, extending into the dirt.

It all seemed tied together and then anchored to his house in some way. He felt a small level of frustration rise in him; he wanted to *understand* this! He still didn't get how Marcus could be so short sighted. This was power, protection from what wanted to harm them all. But yet, forbidden somehow. All Oakheart had said was a small group believed that using magic was wrong, but here they were thousand years later, and no idea how to use the power granted to them.

Heather settled her shoulders and turned back to the house.

"There. Good for the night." Flashing Cendan a smile, she brushed past him, smelling of something sweet or spicy; he couldn't put his finger on it.

Smelling her? Cendan mentally smacked himself. Stay focused he told a fairly distracted part of his mind.

"What does it do? I mean, I saw the layers. No idea what it means though." He closed and locked the door behind them as he followed her inside.

"Really? A basic ward?" Heather was already sitting on the couch, was it his imagination or was she posing a bit?

"Yeah, no idea. Bridgefinder remember? And a new one at that. Magic forbidden." He sat down in a padded chair near her, but kept a bit of distance. She seemed trustworthy enough, but she was a witch after all.

With a glance skyward, Heather gave off a sigh. "I know, Ok fine. Ward has three layers. Green is a general deterrent. It makes people getting too close not want to be close. It basically keeps anyone or anything from randomly wandering into the area being warded. Red is the alarm; if something pushes through which means they *want* to be there, it will wake me. Blue, blue is the actual protection, and if something makes it that far, the red, the last layer will harden like concrete."

"I get it. Green keeps the riff raff away, red alerts you to non-riff raff and blue stops them while you come deal with it." He nodded his approval. It was a simple and nice system, and it made sense, just the way he liked it. "Ok well, now that we are 'warded' and the door is locked; I don't have much to eat here, just some canned stuff. I hadn't been expecting to stay the night.

There's a bathroom and guest room off that door there. I think there's shampoo and stuff, and towels are in the closet."

Heather stood, "Aren't you going to give me the grand tour?"

Cendan, who had been heading towards the kitchen, paused at this. What was her game? Was she trying to... No, stop thinking that way. Focus.

"OK... I... Sure." Swinging his hands around. "Living room." Pointing down the hall lined with books, "Office and library." Turning again, he pointed to the same door he had just pointed out. "Guest room and guest bathroom." Turning back to the way he had been going. "Kitchen, mudroom and garage."

Finally, hooking his thumb towards the stairs, "My room, bathroom, more library, two empty rooms and an unused bathroom. Tour done!" He could feel her irritation from behind him as he made his way into the kitchen and opened the pantry.

"All I have is soup it looks like! I do have some crackers though." He called out to Heather in the living room. Silence greeted him. "Heather?" he called out again, and turned to head back to the living room.

Heather was standing there, in the kitchen, leaning against the archway that lead into the living room.

"Fine, but don't we have something else to do first?"

Desire rushed into him in a torrent. Dimly, he was aware of the fact that this must be a spell. She's casting some sort of mind control, or love spell. He could feel the roaring in his ears and blood rushed past them, a slight tightness in his chest. He had already been attracted to her, but now, she was... stunning. She walked towards him slowly, her lips already in a small smile.

"Cendan Key, do you like me?" a fake coquettish voice asked as she batted her eyes at him.

He tried to speak, to tell her to stop, knock it off, but he couldn't. Her eyes; the curve of her face. His body responded to her walking towards him as she moved closer. Dimly, he nodded. Of course he did, she was beautiful.

"Kiss me Cendan." Her voice seemed to reverberate in his skull; he couldn't think of anything else. He leaned forward as she rose up to meet him. Lips met as fire rushed through him and thought became impossible.

Chapter 8

Morning came to find Cendan groggy and unclear. Sitting up in bed, he headed towards the bathroom to wash his face and stop the odd pounding in his ears. The cold water helped some, but he still couldn't put a finger on why he felt so tired, so off.

"I feel like I'm hung over." Cendan said to his reflection. He'd only been hung over once in his life, a feeling he hated so he'd never done it again. He vaguely remembered it feeling something like this.

Cold realization crossed his mind, accompanied by a wave of goose bumps forming up and down his arms. Heather. Turning towards the bed, he gulped and saw… nothing. No Heather. The bed was a mess to be sure, but it was always a bit of one; he tossed and turned a lot. Maybe it had been a dream? Some sort of magic she worked on him for her own reasons? He searched the bed and found nothing, not even a stray red hair, or a blue one for that matter.

"What would Jasmine say?" he wondered as he sat on the edge of the bed, trying to remember the evening. Immediately he discounted the thought. He and Jasmine were just friends now, they had no claim on the other. But still in the back of his mind, he felt himself uncertain on that point.

Confused, but feeling somewhat calmer, Cendan took a quick shower. He didn't know where Heather was, but he also wasn't sure he was in the right mental state to deal with her. He felt like he needed to center himself, and a good cold shower would do that. The water was bracing, but when he exited, he felt much more like himself, if not a bit hungry and in need of a cup of coffee.

His eyes fell on the bag he had brought from the lair; that much at least seemed consistent with his memories. Marcus had kicked him out, for real. Dressing quickly in shorts and a polo, he made his way downstairs somewhat slowly, looking out for the witch. There was no sign of her anywhere, however, which just made him more puzzled than relieved. He wasn't exactly worried. Truthfully, he considered worry to be a useless emotion in most cases.

But this was strange. Mentally, he recounted what he could to himself. He remembered the wards, then soup, Heather walking towards him, then a kiss… And that was it. It faded off after that, like looking through frosted glass. He could imagine what had happened after, and maybe he could remember it, but was it just his imagination trying to fill in the gap in his mind?

Wards. Were they still there? Had he imagined those as well? Stepping out on his front porch, he brought forth his sight, and there in front of him still were the wards. Slightly less bright than last night, but he sort of remembered it being said they would last for twenty-four hours – so until dusk today. With one last look at the wards, he went inside and made himself some coffee.

Listening to the sound of the coffee-Maker working, he found himself at a bit of a loss. Heather had been here, the wards were proof enough of that. Marcus had kicked him out of the Bridgefinders – his head felt well now, or at least somewhat normal. Something had happened with Heather last night, he was sure of it, but what or how was the question.

Coffee in hand, he headed to the office. He didn't enjoy this sense of not knowing things or understanding what had happened. Sitting in his office, maybe, would calm his mind down some and help him concentrate better. Every time he tried to remember what happened after the kiss, his mind sort of slipped away. It was highly frustrating. His office seemed normal if a bit foreign to him now. Settling into his chair, he flipped on the computer and sipped his coffee, looking out the window onto the garden outside.

Garden. He would miss the garden in the Bridgefinders' lair; some of those plants had been fascinating, and he'd barely scratched the surface of what was there and what they could do. In his heart he had little hope that Jasmine could change Marcus's mind. That didn't mean, however, he was going to give this up. He may be here, but he had his focus, some of the journals, and his powers, even though he wasn't sure what he could do with them.

Grellnot and the Slyph were the real problem, not Marcus and not Heather. If Marcus didn't want him around and those two weren't in the picture anymore, he'd be fine with it. Not happy maybe, but fine. Still, last night bothered him a great deal. And the growing awareness that EVA, while in his head still as a presence, couldn't seem to talk to him at all now.

If he had to describe it, it was as if someone had wrapped that little nodule of thought that was EVA in cotton, then put it inside a bag. He had no idea how or why, and he wasn't going to be able to figure it out, not from here. Cendan sighed at the fact that the list of things he couldn't do anything about kept getting longer. Marcus. EVA. The Map. All of them, things on the list.

The Elves were still there too, waiting for him to find a way into our world. Fun times indeed, he thought with a snort. If he was going to be at home for a while, he needed to do a few things first. Mostly buy groceries. He also considered restarting his work and going consulting again. Oddly enough the idea didn't particularly appeal to him. His bank accounts were still fat, so he didn't need the money. He knew in his heart the reason was simple; his old life seemed so grey to him now. Grey, cold and lonely.

He took a long sip of coffee and shook off some of his melancholy. Sitting here pondering everything he couldn't do wasn't going to get anything done; it just wasted time. As much as Cendan had changed, he still found that unpleasant. Action it was. Quickly getting his wallet, Cendan also took his Key out of his bag.

As usual, the feeling of its warmth and weight gave him some clarity of purpose. A slight tension he hadn't been consciously aware of left him as-well.

"I guess I should keep you with me." Cendan said out loud.

"Well that's good." Heather's voice came from behind him.

Cendan spun around, somewhat surprised.

"Heather! Um... Where have you been?" Oddly he felt himself somewhat embarrassed in front of her. What had happened last night?

"I went to the store of course. Took your car to. Sorry about that." The look on her face was anything but sorry, however. She was enjoying this, him not talking about what the true subject in the room was.

"So...." Cendan paused. "OK I'll say it; what exactly happened last night?"

Heather grinned at him. Grinned! And with a bit of a dramatic flourish, spun away and headed down the stairs. As she walked her voice called out

"What do you think happened?"

Cendan frowned. He didn't these games. He wasn't completely ignorant of this kind of stuff, but he'd never enjoyed this game. It was one reason he had a hard time with relationships. Banter seemed silly to him.

Following her down the stairs, Cendan found her in the kitchen putting a few items away. But not that many; not enough for a stay of any real length.

"I mean it, what happened?" He tried to put some sort of edge in his voice as if he was angry. He wasn't, he was confused, and felt out of his element. "Heather, I remember kissing you and that's all... The rest just sort of slides away."

She sighed and tossed her hair back as she put it in a ponytail with one of those hair things that women always seemed to keep somewhere.

"Does it matter?" Heather asked him as she worked. "I mean, if we did, or we didn't, does it matter?"

Cendan frowned. Of course it mattered.

"Yes, it does. Look, there obviously was magic involved, and if you cast some sort of spell on me to make me do that... I don't like that idea at all."

Eyebrow arched, Heather looked at him.

"You know, Cendan, most men wouldn't be all mad about this. You and I had a very, very good time last night. Surprisingly good in fact."

"Did you use magic to make me sleep with you?" Cendan kept his tone flat. He was getting angry now, the embarrassment fading into irritation and anger.

Heather rolled her eyes. "No, not really. I did, however, use a touch of magic to enhance feelings that were already there. On both of us. It doesn't make you do anything, but it amplifies attraction, desire if, and only if, that attraction is already there. We both were attracted to each other on some level. I just sped things along a bit."

Silence fell and Cendan considered this. Logically, she was correct. He was attracted to her. She was striking, intelligent, and tough. All qualities he found attractive. But the idea of using magic to 'speed things along' as Heather put it wasn't cool. He didn't like that idea at all.

"So you're saying you basically used magic to mimic the effect of giving me too much to drink?"

Heather eyed him with a somewhat surprised expression.

"You're unhappy about this? You were interested; I was interested. It would have happened anyway, at some point."

Heather cleared her throat. "Does this have anything to do with that other Bridgefinder, Jasmine?"

Cendan shook his head, disgust and annoyance shutting down any lingering traces of attraction. "No. This does not." The words shot out of his mouth.

"Then what the hell is the problem?" Heather sighed, stretching and leaning against the kitchen counter.

Feeling his skin crawl, Cendan shot her a look of disgust.

"It's wrong! If I want to do that, I want to be in control of it. Not under the influence of some charm."

"Ok fine. You're overreacting, though." With an eye-roll, she went back to putting away the few things she had got at the store. "So, Breakfast?"

Cendan looked at her with new eyes. She really didn't understand his disgust with her actions. To her, using magic to get what she wanted was second nature. To him, it was wrong all over. Wrong to use people; wrong to use magic; just wrong. Maybe this was the reason that the group of Bridgefinders had walked away from magic.

It was so easy to do things like this; change people; manipulate things. You lose sight of what life is like for those who can't do magic. Having that tool, one could change everything and everyone around you, based on your whims. For once he could see why people would be afraid of that. Without some kind of moral compass, without some grounding, it would be far too easy to treat everyone else like a toy, something to use and then walk away from.

That didn't mean he agreed with the idea that magic was evil or wrong, or whatever idea it was that people like Marcus had. Magic was a tool. A powerful, awesome tool. Put a powerful tool in the hands of someone who was a sociopath, and there are problems, potentially huge ones. That same tool in the hands of someone who has some moral center, someone who wants to help others, and you get a very different outcome.

Heather had grown up with magic. Her whole life, it had been there for her to use, and use it she had. To her, getting what she wanted with it was as normal as breathing air. It didn't make what she had done to him right, but it made sense. It also meant he needed to be prepared for more of it. If not from her, then from the others like her. He was still going to go with her to meet these other users of magic. Whatever the moral compasses, he needed knowledge and training; training he wasn't going to get at the lair. The books didn't really cover much, and Oakheart's knowledge in his focus was short of details in a lot of subjects.

"Breakfast, I said?" Heather asked again, the edge of annoyance in her voice becoming more pronounced.

"Yeah sure." Cendan answered, his stomach reminding him that on top of anything else, he was hungry.

A fast meal later, Cendan found himself ready to face whatever it was Heather wanted to show him.

"Ok, let's go meet these people. Or place... You've not been clear, you know," he asked Heather, carefully keeping his magic sight open, and his focus in his pocket. He wasn't sure what good it would do him, but if she tried to cast something on him unexpectedly, he hoped he could do something back if he had the focus with him.

"Ok, but let me warn you. The place we are going; it may shock you a bit. More than a bit." Heather answered. "And if you got mad about what I did; that was very mild compared to things that have happened there."

His brow wrinkled at this piece of information. "Is it safe Heather?" Cendan had no desire to end up some plaything of anyone.

"Safety is relative. I'll say this. Stay with me, *do not wander off*, and we should be fairly protected." Heather looked at him. "I could cast a spell to help protect you—"

Cendan cut her off, "No!" He swallowed and continued, quieter now. "No. No spells. No using magic on me."

Heather somehow made the thumbs up she flashed look sarcastic as they cleaned up the kitchen and headed toward the car.

"So, where do I drive to?" Cendan asked, trying to put last night and this morning behind him.

"Just head out of town bearing west, towards the mountains. I'll tell you where and when to turn." Her voice continued to show that edge of annoyance. He found it still somewhat surprising that she was annoyed. She had taken advantage of him; he was the one who should be annoyed, not her. Truthfully, he should be far more than annoyed.

The drive was silent. Whatever banter or beginnings of friendship there had been yesterday didn't seem to be there now. That may be for the best though, his inner voice told him. Let it go and concentrate on what needs to happen. One, learn enough to fix the map; two, figure out how to deal with the elves; three, deal with the Grellnot-Slyph war. And finally, what the hell to do about Marcus?

Not a small order, he knew. And he was painfully short on allies. Jasmine he could count on, but she was back in the lair trying to figure out what was going on with Marcus. Sal was dead. He had hoped to rely on Heather, but he didn't trust her now. Sure her self-interest still made it possible to use her to help fix parts of this, namely the Grellnot-Slyph problem. But she couldn't care less about the map, at least for now. Or his elven issue, which she seemed to find amusing. The silence in the car kept leading him to think, and that led back to last night. The more he dwelt on it, the more he didn't like it. Finally, as he sat driving and stewing in his disgust and anger, Heather's voice snapped him back to the now.

"Next left turn; take it."

The road she pointed out was unpaved and looked abandoned.

"You sure? That doesn't look like anything." Cendan noted.

"That's the point. You want a big sign saying, we practice magic here? Sitting on the side of the road," she shot back.

The road was rougher than it appeared, Cendan wincing slightly at the ride. His car wasn't really meant for this kind of off-road work. The road ahead snaked back and forth, leading deeper into the mountains. They were in a forest now, the overarching branches blocking a fair amount of sunlight, making for a somewhat dimly - lit green tunnel.

Finally, Heather pointed to a slight spur where he could pull his car over.

"Park here. From this point we walk." Now her voice was almost cold towards him, which kind of suited him fine now. Allies, but not friends. Maybe that was the best way to be with her. And whoever else they met in this place.

As he exited the car, he opened himself up to the magic sight and nearly gave a gasp of surprise. The motes of light he associated with magic here, were thick. Very thick, and in constant motion. Nearly tsunami sized waves and gusts of it flowed around them, doing what he didn't know.

He grasped his focus in his pocket in an almost involuntary response. That calmed him a bit, but he still couldn't begin to make sense of what he was seeing.

"Impressive isn't it? It's part of the wards. Here they are permanent. Your Bridgefinders have your headquarters, which is something to behold, but here we have our place. Our place for this entire continent, at least." Heather gave a smirk again, and Cendan felt his irritation with her rise again. Her superior attitude did her no favors.

Chapter 9

"So, what's the name of this place?" Cendan asked, watching the magic flow around them as they strolled down a narrow path that Heather had started down first.

"Let's make sure they let you in first. Then I'll tell you." Heather answered back.

The air had gotten somewhat cooler surprisingly, with the light getting even dimmer. Heather paused and took her fetish off her wrist, and with a wave it started to glow, casting a blue-white light around her.

"Don't want you to trip," she called over her shoulder.

Cendan, who had kept himself open to the magic sight, noted how the motes caused the light to form on her fetish. He felt reasonably confident that he could replicate that. At least he was learning more about magic from her, regardless of her flaws as a person.

Stopping in a small clearing between two huge trees, Heather held up one hand to Cendan. The air was cooler still, here. Cendan, clad in a polo shirt and shorts, was starting to get downright uncomfortable. It was dark here as-well. Only with his magic sight could he see the motes forming a wall here, impossibly high and strong. The two trees formed some sort of gate though it didn't make a lot of sense to him. It was similar in feeling to the barrier into the Bridgefinders' lair, but not the same; not exactly.

If he had to pick a word, it was that the Bridgefinders' gate to the lair felt more mechanical, created, and manmade. This felt organic, grown, and part of the world itself. They stood in silence, but Cendan watched as the motes flew around them both, landing on Heather and himself. He couldn't feel anything when they touched him though he wondered if he should.

Finally, after a good ten minutes of standing in the cold and dark, lit only by Heather's fetish, they heard footsteps. Coming between the two trees in front of them.

Heather whispered to Cendan, "Don't say anything unless you're asked a question directly. Let me do the talking here. And turn off your magic sight. We don't want to annoy anyone."

Cendan reluctantly let go of the sight, and the world seemed lesser, somehow.

A man stepped into the pool of light and looked at them with recognition at Heather firstly and then surprise at himself. The man was tall and thin. A neat trimmed beard with a few streaks of red mixed into the… What color was that? Dark brown? Black? It was hard to tell in this light.

"Heather, welcome back. And you've brought someone. Why do I think that you didn't tell anyone of this?"

The man's voice was the largest surprise; Cendan had never heard a voice that deep before. It seemed to almost creak out of him, deep and somehow part of something greater.

"Greengate, I brought him because he needs knowledge. He has great power, but no way of knowing how to use it." She kept her eyes locked forward, not exactly looking at the figure in front of her.

Greengate? What kind of name was that, Cendan mused? Ceremonial? Some sort of guard, maybe?

Heather spoke up once more. "And yes, the Eldest of the Elders; he knows. It was a possibility at least." Greengate didn't respond verbally, but gave her a small nod in response.

Greengate approached him, and Cendan was washed over with the feelings of loam and earth, water and air, and ancient power; very old and very strong. Greengate looked at him with eyes as green as new spring leaves. Cendan couldn't help but wonder what this man looked like with his magic sight, but he reluctantly kept his sense firmly in the mundane world.

Greengate gave him a long hard look, then whirled towards Heather.

"A Bridgefinder? You brought a Bridgefinder here?"

Heather sighed. "He got kicked out. Look, I can explain to the Elders. All I have done, I've done to protect us and this world. You know what's happening on the Echo World?"

Greengate looked back at Cendan. "Tell me, Bridgefinder, why do you think you are here?"

"Honestly... I am not entirely sure. Learn about magic, maybe? The Bridgefinders; they lost it. Lost their knowledge of it." Cendan answered back, finding himself highly unsure of how much detail he should go into. Quickly deciding that honesty was the best policy, he continued. "Without that knowledge, without the skills on how to work magic, or make things with it, the Slyph or Grellnot will win. And I don't think anyone truly wants that."

Greengate looked at him silently for a few moments, motionless except for a few stray hairs on his head, moving as if brushed by a breeze.

"Heather, why did you bring him here?" he asked, his voice breaking the silence. The air was still in the clearing, but it was even colder now. How had this man's hair been moving? There wasn't any wind down here.

"I brought him here to learn; that much is true. He's a creator, an untrained one, but the first to be a Bridgefinder since their last one got captured by the Slyph." Pointing to Cendan but keeping her eyes on Greengate, she continued, "He went to the Echo world, in the flesh. Found the last Bridgefinder creator and got what knowledge he could. But he needs more, far more if he or the Bridgefinders are going to be any help."

Greengate's eyebrows arched a bit at this news.

"You went to the Echo World, Bridgefinder? You met Oakheart? Interesting trip, indeed." Greengate walked a circle around them, his steps, oddly, making no sound at all. "You, Bridgefinder, are a bit of a puzzle. You say you want to learn from us... The people your group disavow. Unlike the Bridgefinders, we exist in a delicate dance with the Slyph. Using magic and her creatures to get what we want. You just want it gone." Greengate paused in-between the two huge trees that dominated the clearing, his hair fluttering again in a way that reminded Cendan of leaves in the wind. If there was any wind. Why did he keep thinking that?

"Normally, I'd not allow you to enter. There are reasons we keep ourselves hidden from you Bridgefinders. But the upcoming war between the Slyph and that infernal creature Grellnot changes a great many things. There is no dance with Grellnot, only death. So I will let you pass. I know Heather says you were kicked out, but the mark of the Bridgefinders is still upon you. I can sense it."

Holding up a hand to stop any questions, Greengate continued. "Your questions, Bridgefinder, will be answered past me." Greengate turned his attention to Heather, his eyes shrouded in the dim light. "Heather, he is your responsibility. Take him to the Elders immediately. They will decide what to do. I'm just a guard."

Greengate looked at Cendan one more time, almost saying something before closing his mouth and walking back the way he entered, between the two huge trees in front of them. His steps once more made a soft rustle that quickly faded out of earshot.

"Who was that?" Cendan asked, unnerved by the whole thing.

"That was the Greengate, the guardian of the way in and out." Heather answered with a shrug. "A gatekeeper, protector. Serious, but what can you expect from a tree."

Cendan looked at her with some surprise. "A tree?"

Heather pointed at the two trees in front of them. "Sorry, trees. Greengate is a magical creation. He lives and is a living part of those two trees. When they die, he dies. He's been the guard here for eight hundred years so far."

Cendan took this in before blurting out a question. "His hair... It moved like leaves in the wind…"

Heather gave a small nod. "Yes. The tops of the trees are being blown up above the forest. Sometimes, what happens to the trees causes a small effect on Greengate."

"He seemed, human, but odd. But I guess that explains it. What did he mean by mark of the Bridgefinders?" Cendan hadn't felt any mark upon him and when he had joined. He had simply put his key in the barrier room. Nothing crazy.

"No idea. But the Elders can say more," Heather answered before turning to Cendan, her face, for once, lacking a trace of sarcasm or annoyance. "Look, Cendan, you're about to enter a place that is special. Very special. This is one of the seven sacred places of our kind in the world. And yes, it's here for a reason, since you Bridgefinders built your machines and made all the Bridges come here, mostly."

"Forget what you heard about us. This is the truth. There are far more of us than the Bridgefinders know. We keep that information a secret. While the Bridgefinders use magic with machinery, and human knowledge, we use magic with nature, and the rules of the Green. Even the name we call each other is kept hidden."

Heather took him by the hand as they walked in-between the trees. Cendan felt a sensation similar to the Bridgefinders lair door, but somehow different, like a familiar song played in a slightly different key.

People. Far more than he expected greeted his sight. Thirty; forty; who knew? A wood of carefully spaced trees spread out before him as sunlight streamed down. He held an involuntary hand up to shade his face.

"We are the Shrouded, Cendan Key, and welcome to Rivenwood." Heather smiled she was home.

Chapter 10

Grellnot stood in front of the Jabber headman, trying not to react to the mix of noises coming from the creature. Jabbers were loud but powerful creatures, large and strong but not terribly smart. With a voice like the wind howling through a thousand pipes, the leader of this tribe of Jabbers spoke.

"Youuu wanntt us to side with yoooouu? Against the mistress who created usssss? Against the Slyph?" The thing shifted from side to side, its many mouths breathing and smacking as it waited for Grellnot to respond.

"Yes. She has an army. Grellnot needs one too. You side with me, Grellnot let you and your tribe live. You do not, and Grellnot will eat every Jabber child and woman here. You will watch your tribe die slowly." Grellnot grinned at the Jabber Headman. Jabbers didn't taste great, too many teeth for Grellnot's liking with all those mouths covering their bodies. But killing them and taking a few bites out of each would have the same effect.

"Yooouuu can't do that to all of usssss. Yoooouuu are smallll... and we are noooot." The Jabber headman crossed its arms over its chest, the mouths facing Grellnot making spitting noises. Grellnot grinned and leapt at a Jabber doing something with a pot. His teeth ripped out its throat before any of the other Jabbers could react. Grellnot reached into the raw wound and pulled out a piece, eating it in a highly exaggerated fashion.

"Grellnot does what Grellnot says. Your tribe is large, and Grellnot is always hungry."

It watched the Jabber chief, as half its mouths sputtered and mumbled, and the other moaned in alarm. Slowly each mouth shut, in what Grellnot assumed was thought.

"Well? Grellnot either feasts or you serve Grellnot. Either way, Grellnot wins." Taking its clawed hand, now blood covered with gore, Grellnot wiped it on its filthy clothing.

"Sheeeee created ussssss…. Sheeee made you…. Littllee foooouuullll thing…" The Jabber's voice answered back finally. "Whhhyyyy do youuuu want to fiiigghtt her..?"

Grellnot spat. "She always gets what she wants. Grellnot wants to be free of her, and Grellnot wants to feast on her. All that magic, all that power, Grellnot needs it!" Screaming at the end, Grellnot bounded towards a young Jabber, not even five feet tall yet.

"Noooooooooo!" the Jabber chief wailed. "Weeeee will.." It paused as every mouth on its body swallowed at once. "We willll serrveee youuuuu."

Grellnot grinned, knocking over the young Jabber that screamed in terror through every mouth. "Shut up!" Grellnot screamed at it as silence fell.

"Grellnot accepts. Come to the ruins of Oakheart when Grellnot tells you to come. You will know. Come, or Grellnot will hunt every member of your tribe down. You cannot hide from Grellnot."

Its stomach rumbled as Grellnot wondered if young Jabber tasted better than older ones. Grellnot knew, however, that it shouldn't push too hard, yet. After these stupid creatures and the others it would gather fulfilled their purpose, everything on this world, and the humans' world, would exist for one reason. To fill its hunger.

Jasmine sat in the stillness and quiet of the kitchen, trying to figure out how to broach the subject of Cendan with Marcus. Marcus. She'd known the man for years, her whole life basically. They'd grown up together in many ways, both children of the Bridgefinders. After everything that had happened with the map and Cendan, however, she wasn't sure she understood him at all.

She'd long known that Marcus was a proud man. Proud to be a Bridgefinder, to dedicate his life to protecting the world, even if the world didn't know that he existed. Proud to be the leader of a dying order. He'd even, at first, been proud to have been the man who found a Maker again. But his pride had soured, and quickly.

How had it all gone so south? How had he convinced himself that Cendan of all people, bland and boring Cendan, was the true enemy? Sal's death; had that pushed him over the edge? Or was it before that? He'd not been happy to find out that Cendan had kept his Maker status a secret from them, and truthfully she'd seen the momentary pain on his face when he'd realized that she and Cendan had dated once.

Marcus had long been interested in her as more than a friend. The attraction, however, wasn't mutual, if only because she had always felt like his interest was based only on the idea that as 'children of Bridgefinders', they should 'just be together.' When they were both younger, Marcus had gotten rip-roaring drunk once, and in an only semi-coherent rant gone off about how their kids would be the most powerful Bridgefinders ever.

Jasmine wanted nothing to do with that. It made her feel like some sort of breeding animal, and she'd told him so. He'd mumbled something about time and never mentioned it again, but she often wondered if he remembered what he'd said. But somewhere in the last few weeks, sitting by himself, Marcus had changed, his pride and joy at turning the tables on the Slyph, morphing into anger and jealousy.

She had to try to talk to him, and there was only one place he would be; the same place he always was. The barrier room. Her footsteps echoed down the empty halls of the headquarters, feeling even sparser than it had when there were just four of them. Unless there was some way to fix this, the Bridgefinders would be dead. All that history, all that work, lost. Lost for the sake of pride.

Standing in front of the door, there were only two lights left; hers and Marcus's. The sight of all those blank spaces, all those turned off lights, depressed her. Taking a deep breath, Jasmine readied herself. This wasn't going to be a fun conversation. She wasn't sure what to expect from him, but if his behavior yesterday was any guide, she didn't think it would be a normal one.

Pushing the door open, the room seemed colder than normal to her. She'd not been in the room for over a week or so; there hadn't been much need, truthfully, with not having to run off and close Bridges. So she was somewhat thrown by its new appearance.

The chairs were the first thing. Before, the room had been somewhat haphazard, the chairs thrown about in chaos, most dusty and unused. Marcus, however, had been apparently busy. Now, all of them, several hundred chairs by her guess, were organized smallest to largest, all facing the center of the room and the barrier wall with its empty depressions. The room had always been rather dimly lit, but now it was even more so, one candle in the middle and one in each corner. And finally, there was now a chair in the middle of the room.

There had always been a place for one there. Her mother had once shown her a painting of a meeting in this very room when the Bridgefinders had been many and strong. The middle position was taken by the leader of the Bridgefinders. For a moment she wondered where that picture was now. Buried in some storeroom, she figured; out of sight and out of mind.

Marcus, apparently, had seen that picture before as well, as he was now sitting in that chair, facing away from the door once more. It was his right to do so of course; he was the leader. Of course, he'd only been the leader because she'd had no interest in what to her seemed a ceremonial position. When there were only a handful of people left, and they all did the same job who cared who was the 'leader'? Marcus had been all excited about it, however, and so, she'd let him have it.

"Hello Jasmine." Marcus's voice echoed in the quiet chamber. "I figured you'd be here at some point." He didn't get up or face her, nor even shift in his seat from what she could see. "You're here to discuss yesterday, I assume? When that betrayer of your ex-boyfriend destroyed what was left of us."

Jasmine sighed. She'd known that it was going to be a fun conversation, but this was already bad and she hadn't even said anything yet.

"Marcus, Cendan didn't do anything—"

Before she could speak, Marcus's fist slammed down on the chair's arm.

"He did! If he hadn't come here, Sal would be alive, the map would still be working, and you wouldn't be mixed up in his dangerous ideas about magic!" Marcus paused for a second, and pulled a large sphere from somewhere that Jasmine couldn't see. "Jasmine, he's dangerous. At first... at first I was blinded by the idea of a Maker. A real Maker. Here. Finally. Fix EVA, discover all these things that we didn't understand about this place. And most importantly, turn the tide on the Slyph and her creatures."

Silence ruled for a few seconds as he appeared to gather his thoughts.

"I wanted to like him. Cendan Key. Even his name is stupid." Holding the sphere up, Marcus appeared to look at it. "But after Sal died, and EVA was online for the first time in a thousand years, I came here to think. Think and explore. I realized, Jasmine, that Cendan is nothing but poison."

"I am the leader of the Bridgefinders, Jasmine. Me. Not you, not Cendan, me. You always thought it was a joke, I know. A position of a figurehead. But it's not. And it never was." Marcus held the sphere in his hand up in the dim light. "I'd imagine you're curious as to what this is. This is my birthright. The legacy of all the leaders of the past."

Suddenly, Marcus stood and faced Jasmine. She was taken aback by his appearance. A severe looking man, he seemed more gaunt than normal, and in the faint light somewhat maniacal. He continued his speech.

"After Cendan opened the Maker wing, the only good thing he ever did here, I went in and explored. On my own. And I found this. This, Jasmine, is power. This allows me to control almost everything in this place."

"It took me a while to figure it out. The power this gives me dwarfs anything Cendan Key can do. I don't need to sleep, I don't need to eat. THIS!" Marcus raised up the stone in his hand. "THIS sustains me. With this I can work miracles. And its power is mine. Just mine."

Jasmine watched as Marcus started the stone orb, the look of naked ambition obvious on his face. Marcus, eyes narrowed raised his head to watch her, almost studying her.

"With this I have cut-off that pretend Bridgefinder from EVA. Not totally perhaps, not yet, but she can't help him anymore. With this I've banished him from ever coming back in. This Keystone, this is my power." Marcus's face took on an even darker cast as he looked at her. "With this, I even know that you and Cendan weren't alone in the map room yesterday. Who was she, Jasmine? Why did you betray me?" Marcus voice was a harsh whisper. "Once, I would have given you the world. But here you are now… tainted."

He took a step towards her, holding the Keystone out to her.

"Tainted by that pretender, Cendan. He doesn't care about us. He doesn't care about the struggle. He isn't one of us."

Taking another step, Marcus came into closer focus in the dim light. His eyes were bloodshot. When had he slept last, she wondered? He continued to speak.

"He came here, he killed Sal, and he tainted you with his talk of magic. He betrayed my confidence when I made him a Bridgefinder."

"Now, Jasmine, you're going to tell me who that person was with you. You're going to tell me what you had planned. You're going to tell me everything."

Marcus held the Keystone higher as Jasmine felt something pull at her very soul; hard, painful and fast. Before she could get a word out, the world spun around her as she half heard Marcus say,

"I didn't say you would be conscious."

Chapter 11

"Rivenwood? Shrouded?" Cendan asked a bit confused by the terms. The sight before his eyes, however, was one he never would have imagined when he agreed to come here. Rows of huge trees, different types and species, laid before him. The air was cool, but pleasant. A far cry from the oppressive cold and dark of the clearing where they had been questioned by Greengate. Walking around, sometimes in conversation and sometimes in front of a tree touching it, were the oddest assortment of people.

Wild forms of dress, hair colors, and races; none of them looked alike. He actually felt out of place in his plain utilitarian shorts and t-shirt. Those trees struck a chord though. Something nagged at him in the back of his mind; why did this seem familiar?

"Yes, the Rivenwood. And Shrouded is the name we give ourselves. As you can see, there are far more of us than we typically let on. We all vary in power and ability, but this place is... sacred." Heather's voice took his attention away from what he was seeing.

"I get that. So Marcus and Jasmine were wrong. Very wrong." Cendan knew that Marcus would lose it if he knew about this place, not that he hadn't already lost it.

"Yes. As I said, we call ourselves the Shrouded. We hide our numbers from you all, and from... others. Though, after what I've seen, I think the Bridgefinders need to be the ones who hide from us." Her voice betrayed the slight contempt that accompanied that statement.

The truth was she may be right, Cendan told himself. Just in his current view, there were ten, fifteen, perhaps twenty people. If all of them had some ability that was already far more than the Bridgefinders had been at for over a century.

"But you all didn't have Grellnot hunting you down," Cendan answered by way of defense. "Does the Slyph know about you all? Grellnot? This can't stay hidden from them, right?" His question made Heather shrug in response, though he caught a glimpse of irritation, or perhaps anger, at the question.

"The Slyph knows of us ... somewhat. But since we aren't in her face, so to speak, trying to send her minions back, she doesn't deal with us; not directly. As for Grellnot, he leaves us alone unless one of us gets in his way. Or at least that had been the way it had gone until the war on the Echo world broke out." Heather beckoned Cendan to follow her as they walked towards the wood in front of them.

As they passed the other people in this place, some nodded to Heather in passing. They all seemed to totally ignore Cendan for the most part though one man wearing black leather and what looked like tribal tattoos gave him a long hard look. Unsettled, Cendan kept his eyes on Heather from then on, feeling like one hell of an outsider.

"I guess I don't understand. Are you helping the Slyph? Or fighting against her?" Cendan asked as they walked through the trees. "I know you all deal with the creatures there. Though I'm unclear as to the nature of those deals and what you actually get out of it."

Heather paused and turned towards him. "Our dealings with the creatures of the Slyph are simply our way of dealing with the Echo World. We aren't helping her, regardless of what the propaganda says. We fight against her in our own way. We just aren't nearly as in your face about it as you all are."

"What's that supposed to mean? You didn't answer the question, you know," Cendan pushed back. His response, however, was met with a sigh as Heather turned back away from him.

"Just follow me. I think he will be able to answer your questions, and more besides. You have been told a version of the truth, and one that isn't terribly complete."

"He? Who's he?" Cendan asked. He knew the whole reason they were here was to meet with the Elders of these people, these Shrouded. Sal would have loved this, Cendan reckoned. He hadn't known Sal all that great when he got killed, but of the others he would have eaten this up. Jasmine would accept it with some prodding. Not fully, but she'd accept it after a while.

And Marcus? He'd deny that it existed, that it was all a trick. Cendan hoped jasmine was ok. He still didn't like that he'd left her there with Marcus. Marcus and Jasmine had been friends a long time, he knew, but with Marcus's current mental state, he felt uneasy about it. Highly uneasy if he thought about it. There wasn't much he could do, however; EVA was still muffled in his head, and Marcus had kicked him out. Who knew if he'd even be able to get back in?

The surrounding trees were larger now, older. The path they walked on was still clearly marked, but unlike the trees before, these often didn't have anyone near them. Cendan noted, however, that while the day was nice, cool, and clear, the air as they walked had a peculiar quality to it that got stronger the deeper into this Rivenwood place they went. A low hum seemed to fill the air; he could feel it on the back of his neck as-well. Strange place indeed, he thought to himself.

Heather, however, didn't seem to notice it or mention it. Her eyes flicked from time to time to this tree or the next, each time looking down, her face set in a bland mask that seemed somewhat unlike her; at least as far as Cendan knew of her thus far. Finally, in the distance, a rather massive tree rose up out of the forest. Grand in scale, it was some variety of evergreen that Cendan wasn't sure of. What was interesting was that at some point the tree had been struck by lightning or something of that nature. Its trunk was partially split halfway up, but it seemed the tree continued to thrive regardless of the damage.

"This *is the* Rivenwood. The tree that this place is named after. It is the first and eldest." Heather pointed to the tree. "Touch the tree, Cendan, and your questions will be answered."

Cendan paused and looked at her, his eyebrows furrowed then rising fast.

"Touch the tree… Wait…" Cendan spun looking at the surrounding trees. "These trees, all of them… they are like Oakheart!"

Heather said nothing, but lowered her head. "You won't be harmed, Cendan. This isn't a trap. Rivenwood can explain better than I can."

Hesitation filled Cendan. If each of these trees were a person trapped in a tree, then these people, these 'Shrouded', were worse than the Slyph herself. The horror of being trapped, powerless for years, centuries even, made his stomach turn.

"How can you say that? All these people trapped forever—"

Heather cut him off with an upraised hand. "This is not a trap. Just touch the tree, and Rivenwood will explain. If you want to leave after that, fine. But at least listen to us!"

Cendan hesitated. Heather didn't seem to be lying. In fact, her voice betrayed her somewhat shocked thought at the idea that the trees were prisons. His eyes fell onto the tree in front of him, mentally comparing it to Oakheart. Both were grand things as far as trees go. This one was taller whereas Oakheart had been wider. The bark on this tree, this Rivenwood, was smooth in a few places. He wondered if that was where people normally touched the tree, communed with it. Or whatever it is that they call it.

He half began to ask Heather, then stopped himself. Useless trivia at this point. He wondered if he should look for the branches on this choice. Heather claimed that was magic, however, some sort of future telling magic. And working magic here and now, well, that might not be the best choice. This was an either or choice. He touches the tree and sees what it was Heather wanted him to see. Or don't touch, and he wasn't sure what exactly then. He'd been shown the inner workings of these people, this group, the Shrouded, whatever they meant by that.

Add to the fact that he had agreed to meet with the 'Elders' of her group. He had expected it to be people, though. Old wizened crones; wizards in cone hats; flowing robes, and that sort of thing. Not a forest of trees inhabited by the souls and minds of witches and the like from long ago. The advantages of the system were obvious. When someone gets too old, put them in a tree and one is able to learn from them, talk to them. The knowledge and power gets passed on for all time.

Oakheart had, however, soured him on this. He'd been tortured by being a tree for all those years, forced to work for the Slyph, and to lend his magic to the creation of horrible monsters and beings. Add to that the fact that the knowledge that Oakheart had shared via the focus was spotty and broken; was that a function of being a tree or was that a function of what the Slyph had used him for?

Heather's sigh broke his thoughts. Her once calm face had taken on more of a cast of impatience as she stood there waiting for him to make his decision. He didn't have much choice; he had to touch it if only for his own knowledge. Lacking any other good choice, however, Cendan reached into his pocket that held his focus, gripping it with that hand. He reached out, his fingers brushed against the bark, and the world spun away from him leaving him standing in an empty black void.

"Hello Cendan Key. I am Rivenwood. First off, before you say anything else, I have to apologize for Heather. She's powerful, but impetuous and too enamored of what she can do without always thinking if she should do it." The voice that spoke to Cendan was warm, gracious, and reminded Cendan of one of those good Shakespearian actors. Very proper, friendly though. It put him at ease almost instantly.

"I can see that. So you're Rivenwood? What was your name before you became a tree? Did you do this willingly? I've seen this before, and that wasn't a good thing!" Cendan wanted to get the big questions over and done with, before trying to figure out what else was going on here.

Sadness came over him like a wave. The sadness of learning of an old friend's death; not raw, but one of melancholy.

"Oakheart. My friend once. Yes, I know of Oakheart. And my name before the tree was Rivenwood, actually. Aethlic Rivenwood. Willingly? Of course. We aren't like the Slyph here. I wasn't forced into this. I can tell you what you want to know or I can just show you, Cendan. Here in this place, I can show you anything and everything. I can fill in all those blank places the Bridgefinders left empty because, honestly, they didn't know anymore."

Cendan paused and considered this. "Why would you do that? From what I gathered from Heather, the Bridgefinders and you all aren't exactly on the best terms. In fact, from their side of things, you are all dangerous fanatics who do horrible things with the creatures of the Slyph, and get power from that."

A low laugh echoed in his mind with those words before Rivenwood answered.

"Yes, I imagine that they would say that sort of thing. The truth is far different. Let me show you from the beginning of it all. From the moment of the creation of the echoes to the Bridgefinders. There is much our wayward brethren have lost. But I will not show you without your approval and acceptance. I'll not do what Heather did physically, but in a mental way."

Cendan started; this tree knew about that?

"Yes, I can read your thoughts, though that machine Oakheart created, that EVA of his, makes it a bit more difficult. The connection between you, though, it is masked somehow, and that makes it easier than it should be. As for Heather, she will be punished for her actions. They were unwarranted and unwanted. Within the Shrouded those things happen, and the younger members seem to accept it for reasons I don't understand. But you being from outside that was a horrible mistake she made."

Rivenwood's voice assumed the role of a teacher now. Cendan could picture this elderly professor type in his mind about to give a lecture of grave importance.

"First, you need to understand Creation, the truth of our world, the Echo worlds, where the Slyph came from, all of it. I gather the Bridgefinders don't remember any of this, knowing how rabidly anti-magic they have become over the years."

"Echo Worlds? As in plural? So there is more than a single Echo?" Cendan jumped at that point. It had bothered him that no one in the Bridgefinders could answer it. With all the effort in getting things working, he also hadn't had time to really research it in the Maker Wing; not that he was going to get a chance to now.

"Yes, Plural. Let me tell you the story of creation, Cendan Key. It will explain some things and raise new ones I'm sure."

Chapter 12

There was silence, just silence. True silence, the kind of silence that almost hurt. And in this silence, this purity of nothing, a light bloomed. The silence still reigned, but it was different now. Instead of an empty silence, it was the silence that comes before something grand, a silence not born of nothing, but one of great anticipation. And then, a sound. A sound that would bring any living thing to tears of pure joy if anything living could have heard it. A single harmonious sound, it lifted, almost caressing the fading silence, a goodbye kiss to what had been, and a joyful retort to the empty of before. A harmony of making; being; creation itself.

That should have been the end of the silence, the end of the nothing. But not all things happen as planned, and as the nothing was replaced in one shining true point of time, it became aware. The power of creation made it even here, and in its creation, it hated the light and it hated the sound. It hated what had replaced it. But it was new, and without power, so it fled. The remnant of what had been. It fled to the farthest points it could, fleeing the expansion, feeling the making.

The nothing fled and knew itself. It had no name, no form, and no thought but one; to return to before. The nothing ran, but always found creation behind it, chasing it. Regardless of how fast the nothing moved, the something was always right there. Eventually, the nothing gave it a name; existence.

The nothing ran for millions of years, and then one day, found a hole. A gap; a break in the creation that had come and displaced it. It was more nothing, but unlike itself, it was not aware. It had not been perverted by the act of creation. The nothing joined with it, and the hole became more, bigger, stronger. The nothing gave itself a name, knowing that as much as it hated creation, it hated that it knew and thought. It called itself Valkith.

Millions of years passed, or only a handful of days, we will never truly know. Dust and gas were created, condensed, and made new things. Suns, planets, rocks, everything. And still Valkith sat in his hole of nothing, hating, seething, and hating itself just as much as it hated what had replaced it. But Valkith was just a mind, a consciousness attached to nothing. In this darkness and hate, a plan came to it. A plan to fix this mistake it saw; creation, light, even itself.

Valkith left its hiding place and was horrified, even roused to greater anger by what it found. Where once there had been the perfect empty void and silence of pure nothing, now there were things everywhere. Matter, gasses, liquids, and even worse; life had started and come to creation. Life that had solid form. Life that bred and continued on. Valkith was stirred to great anger and set forth its plan to unmake it all.

Creation had been a sound, and the sound had echoes. Shadows of what was real populated outward, hidden from each other but close enough to touch if given the right power. Valkith went from world to world, taking tiny bits of itself, fragments of its power and hate, and placing them on these echoes. On each one, its fraction of its formless mind would be different, but each would be driven by the need and want to conquer and destroy the first note of creation.

When it had succeeded, Valkith would then take that fragment into itself and take back its power. No fragment would be able to stop the whole, and so Valkith would step-by-step, and part by part, destroy not only the main note of creation, but all the echoes as well, leaving nothing once more. The perfect empty void.

But Valkith didn't understand creation, and this was its undoing. In the act of giving up the parts of himself to make new life, life that had one purpose, he still created. He made something. And this making perverted him, changed him. As he changed, what he created changed too, until the birth of the Spinner.

The Spinner was created by Valkith in some unknown Echo far down the line. Created to destroy in mind, instead the Spinner chose to protect as best it could. Lacking the power to destroy its siblings, or its parent, the Spinner chose to bind an Echo to another Echo, or in some cases, to the main note of creation. The binding would limit the spread of Valkith as each world it bound would only be able to go between it and the world it was connected to.

The Spinner bound us to the Slyph's World. This is why, while we know of the other Echoes, and can even see them sometimes, we can't open Bridges to them, and they can't come to us. The Spinner is out there still connecting worlds, limiting the spread of the evil and desire for pure nothing that its parent spreads across creation.

Valkith is still out there as well, somewhere. Mutated and changed in ways beyond it ever thought, it still hates creation. What it does now, and where it is, however, is beyond us.

Cendan shuddered. The 'story' as Rivenwood had described it had been words in his mind that had overwhelmed him.

"Valkith? Spinner? So you're saying... the Slyph is one of these fractions of something called Valkith?" Cendan wasn't sure what to make of that. To think that the Slyph, for all her power, was just a fraction of something of far greater power was not something he wanted to contemplate.

"Yes. One that, oddly enough, chose to create herself, she mutated and changed as well. Grellnot, with its ravenous hunger, is closer to the truth of her birth than she is, even if he is a fraction of a fraction of the true power here." Rivenwood paused. "I want to show you more. The next will be something visual as well. This is drawn from memories that were passed down, the split between us; the Shrouded and the Bridgefinders. You need to understand how and why the split happened, and how and why it's important to fix."

Cendan was curious about this; what had happened between these two groups? On the face of it, having both groups aligned would have been a boon beyond measure in the fight against the Slyph.

"Does this involve you and Oakheart?" That interaction between the two of them was another thing he needed to know. At least from this side, once he had a quiet place to work, he was going to search through everything Oakheart had given him on the Key to see if there was any mention of Rivenwood or these Shrouded people.

"No. This happened many years before either of us was born. However, the memories of this event have been passed down, just as Oakheart passed his down to you." Was that a trace of humor in Rivenwood's response?

"Does that strike you as amusing, Rivenwood?" Cendan needed every bit of information he could get, and if Rivenwood found something amusing, he wanted to know why.

"Yes, because the skill to transplant memories and knowledge into a fetish – or as the Bridgefinders call them, a focus – is one that Oakheart got from us. Though, we will get to that. First, let me show you the split."

The two groups faced each other, each looking at a leader. One leader was a man clad in leather and wearing an assortment of tools and equipment on his belt, and in other places. On the other side, a woman, clad in a simple white robe, barefoot and smiling.

"Bandic, reconsider this course. We are one, you know this. The skills and abilities we share are far greater than this silly separation you have started." The woman looked at the man with an appraising look, measuring.

"There is nothing else to say, Rin. There has been nothing left to say for months, even years now. The old ways are fine, but we need a new path, a new way to move forward. Our skills combined with craftsmanship, human skill; those will give us an edge over anything that comes for our world."

Rin sighed, with more than a little frustration. "Bandic. We've covered this. Your craftsmanship is fine, and your followers, but we work in the framework that we've always had; within the natural world, using the power that lives here on our world. We have no quarrel with the Slyph directly. She only seeks to understand us."

Bandic scowled at the name of the Slyph. "That creature is no friend of ours. She has plans and plots within plans and plots. We should close those Bridges into our world as soon as we find them, send her creatures back, and do no traffic with them."

Rin shook her head. "All that would do is antagonize a vastly powerful creature. We keep her and her minions at a distance. We all know that some of her creations are less than friendly, and even the ones she made to be more acceptable to us, they have their own challenges, so to speak."

Bandic spat. "Elves."

"Yes the Elves. But splitting us like this, taking those who would combine craftsmanship and human machinery with the magic of this world and forming a new group... This is wrong. We can work something out."

Bandic sighed and shook his head.

"Rin, we've tried this for three years. Walls go up whenever we try to do something new. Just because something works, doesn't mean there isn't a new way that might be better."

"And just because it's new doesn't mean it is better!" Rin shot back. "You want to leave? Fine, leave. But this group, all these people, Bandic, you're splitting us up!" Rin waved at the crowd behind him. Nearly a third of the people as they called themselves were joining Bandic on his foolish push. Creation with magic was a careful and lengthy process. Materials were shaped for weeks, even months. Magic was used to help push things along, but to use shortcuts and the manual labor of the common man, was an affront to their very core.

"Rin, they come of their own volition. I didn't ask them to join me. Not a single one. The world is changing; people are changing. How we work in the power needs to change along with it." Bandic sighed. "We are not enemies here, Rin. Consider us cousins, family with a different focus. But we will not leave this course, Rin. Not at all, for any reason."

Rin was silent for a long while, then with a long look at Bandic and his assorted followers, she gave a short nod.

"I will hope beyond hope that one day this does not change; that we do not become enemies. Trust me when I say this, however; this step will work more change than you could imagine. I only hope that the end result will be the better for it."

Bandic nodded, but did not respond as he turned and walked away, his followers coming behind him.

Cendan shuddered, feeling cold if that was possible.

"So, Rin and Bandic; that was the start of the Bridgefinders? Bandic started it? What did Rin mean by the end result?"

Rivenwood paused, and all Cendan could do was think that he was mulling his answer over. Talking to a mind living in a tree had its disadvantages; you can't see a face or read any body language.

"Yes. Though the names the Shrouded and Bridgefinders hadn't come yet. Before the split, they called everyone who could use magic simply 'the people'. The other names came later."

"So, the split was because Bandic and his followers wanted to do things in a new way? Nothing wrong with trying something new, Rivenwood." Cendan didn't feel like Bandic had been in the wrong, really.

"Yes, though there was more to it. Bandic and his people didn't trust the Slyph either and favored a much more direct approach to dealing with her. While Rin and the others favored the soft touch, the same way we deal with her today, Bandic led the way to the direct action of closing the Bridges and banishing creatures." The response came back, filling Cendan's mind.

"Good! You and Heather have been less than open about how and what you do with the Echo world." Cendan felt himself get defensive about the Bridgefinders almost as soon as he said it. A more analytical part of his mind found this somewhat amusing; he was attached to them, the Bridgefinders, already it appeared.

"We talk to the creations of the Slyph to find out what she's up to. We draw magical power through those creatures, power of her world in small amounts, and then in trade give the creatures that came through something in return. It's all very equitable, honestly." Rivenwood retorted back.

"What do you give them in return? What could you possibly have that they want?" Cendan asked, his mind instantly going to his Elven problem. "Money? Food? What?"

Rivenwood didn't answer right away, and all Cendan could see in his mind was of a gathering storm, silence hung thick, and he began to wonder if he should break off contact, when Rivenwood finally answered.

"What they want. You need to understand, most of the creations that come through outside your machine's focus are natural ones. Not created by the Slyph. The things that come through don't have an agenda. Sometimes its food, or material goods. Sometimes it's other things."

"What other things?" Cendan wasn't going to let this go. "Rivenwood, tell me. You want me to trust you all? You want me to put what happened last night out of my head? To work with you all? Tell me."

Cendan felt his control slipping a bit. Teeth gritted, he waited for the response.

"Do we send women to the Elves? No, not anymore. Did we in the past? Yes. It's a shameful item from our past. I am not proud of it, and due to your circumstances, not one I wanted to get into. We don't tend to deal with the more aggressive creatures as a whole. Dwarves, gnomes, elves, treans, sprites; those are the things we deal with."

"Treans? Never heard that one." Cendan asked, picking up on the new name.

"Intelligent trees. Not many of them; they weren't aggressive enough for the Slyph to be of much use." Rivenwood responded. "Are your fears answered?"

Cendan pondered the answers he had gotten from Rivenwood.

"Are there any others outside these two groups? Outside the Bridgefinders and the Shrouded?"

Those storm clouds in his mind's eye broke out in lightning at the question.

"Yes. But the less we deal with them, the better. There is no moral compass there; just power. But I still need to show you the final split. Drawn from my own memories. This is almost six hundred years after the initial split. Over the years, the two groups worked together at times, and we were on a somewhat friendly basis. There was even the occasional intermarriage between the two groups." Rivenwood's voice became sad, regretful.

"The two groups, though, became more and more separate over time. We stuck to the old ways, tried and true, simple, and natural. The Bridgefinders became more and more involved with machinery and the craft. They made wondrous things too. The headquarters of the Bridgefinders could never have been made any other way. The machine, EVA, was the near culmination of the craftsmanship and skill they commanded. But something ugly started to take hold in the group. You know what it was." Rivenwood's voice prodded an answer from Cendan.

"The hatred of Magic. The denial of its function and even existence." Cendan answered, feeling where this was going.

"Yes. That group pushed farther, not content with the merging of technology and magic, they wanted to drop the magic part altogether. At the time of the final split, they were a small but vocal group in the Bridgefinders, but eventually, sadly... they prevailed. Which has led directly to where the Bridgefinders are today."

Cendan nodded.

"So what caused the final split? You said it comes from your memories?" Cendan wanted to keep this on topic, and move on.

"Oakheart did, or at least his joining the Bridgefinders did. Oakheart's true name was Mindeth Oakheart. He was born one of us, one of the Shrouded. He was also a Shaper of Things, what you are, what the Bridgefinders call a Maker. Early on, we knew that while he was born to us, his heart lay with them. His skills were amazing, even as a child. He was deft with the power, but craved more than we did here."

Cendan inwardly celebrated the fact that he finally knew Oakheart's real name. At least he could scratch that off his list of things he didn't know about all this.

"So, his leaving was the final straw?" Cendan asked.

"Let me show you, then ask questions." Rivenwood's response came as a vision rushed toward Cendan.

Oakheart stood with his hands holding a large hammer, fidgeting with it as he waited.

"Aethlic my friend, what is the problem?" he asked the figure who was sitting down, leaning against a rock. "You know I don't belong here; they know I don't belong here; everyone knows it. Let me leave and be done with it."

Aethlic Rivenwood sighed. Mindeth Oakheart was his best friend and had been for years. Talented beyond measure, he was however nearly blind to the political and power ramifications of his leaving.

"Oakheart, you know the relations between us and the Bridgefinders have been bad for nearly a hundred years, now. Too many disagreements over how and what to do now that the Slyph has turned aggressive. An aggressive turn that we many find the Bridgefinders at fault for." Aethlic Rivenwood shook his head. Why some had to choose to get into direct confrontation with a super powerful magical entity he didn't understand.

"Good! We should have done that as well. She's untrustworthy, Rivenwood. Mark my words, she wants nothing good for us or our world."

"I didn't say she did, but before the Bridgefinders decided to force things by banishing creatures and closing Bridges, she wasn't outright attacking us. We were managing her, keeping her off guard and off base. Soft power, Oakheart. Now, she creates creatures that are nightmares, creatures that exist to hurt and hunt. To destroy and harm." Rivenwood pointed out.

Oakheart dismissed that with a wave of us hand.

"She would have done that, regardless. At best, the Bridgefinders accelerated the conflict a bit, but better to be prepared and start the conflict on your terms than the enemy's."

Rivenwood sighed. This was an argument that not only had he and Oakheart had many times over the last few years, it was one that had finally driven a wedge between the Shrouded and the Bridgefinders. That wedge was the reason that there were serious misgivings about letting Oakheart leave to join the Bridgefinders. Do you let someone who was as powerful as Oakheart join a side that only seems to seek further confrontation with a thing like the Slyph? Where is the line?

"You are my friend, Oakheart. I mean that. But the Bridgefinders have planted these ideas in your head. This is not the way to survive." Rivenwood tried to be calm about it all, but knew that Oakheart didn't want to listen.

"Aethlic Rivenwood, you are my friend. But this dancing around the Slyph will only lead to further loss. Action must be met with action."

A soft chime roused them both. The Council of Elders had finished their meeting. One elder, named Tern came forth to the clearing where they were. Surprisingly, with him came a much younger woman, clad in leather, looking decidedly pleased with herself. Tern frowned.

"Mindeth Oakheart. You have asked to leave us, the Shrouded and Join the Bridgefinders. To choose the ways of those who were once our family." Tern continued.

Rivenwood stiffened at this choice of words. Once our family?

"We will grant you this." Oakheart's face broke out in a grin, as did the woman who stood with Tern, "but, know this, Oakheart. If you leave with Finioa here and join the Bridgefinders, you may never return to us. We, the leadership of the Shrouded, have placed the edit of separation. The Shrouded and the Bridgefinders are no longer family. We are no longer connected. The split started by Bandic all those years ago is now complete."

The woman Tern had identified as Finioa rolled her eyes at this announcement.

"That was your choice, Tern. You all are just mad that one of your most powerful members is leaving you."

Tern's face scowled at the woman. "We have discussed that until we have nothing else left to say, Finioa."

Rivenwood spoke up. "So you're saying that from this moment on, what... No communication between us and the Bridgefinders?"

"Yes. The names of their members will be stricken from the rolls, and we shall have nothing to do with them henceforth. What was one is now two. This is the final decision of the Elders." Tern tapped his staff against the ground as a wave of magic flew out. As it passed over Rivenwood, he felt a bell ring throughout his body. "Finioa take your new member and leave. You are not welcome here anymore."

Chapter 13

Cendan felt fuzzy headed. All this mind to mind stuff seemed to make him a bit confused.

"So, Oakheart left, joined the Bridgefinders, made EVA and who knows what else, then got captured by the Slyph, turned into a tree thing like you all, and turned into basically a magic battery for the Slyph to use?" He hoped that was a semi accurate summary of everything he knew. Or at least he had been told. Cendan wasn't totally sold that these people, these Shrouded, were telling him everything any more than he had been sure the Bridgefinders had been. People always had their own versions of truth. Without a response, Cendan continued.

"So, if there wasn't supposed to be any contact anymore between the Shrouded and the Bridgefinders, how did Heather get there? Why am I here?" Cendan pushed on. "By everything you've shown me, there aren't a lot of reasons for this conversation to even be happening. Right? I mean, that vision said it; what was one is now two. Period."

"Yes. And it would have stayed that way but for one thing; Grellnot. Grellnot happened. Even Grellnot existing was a high concern for us, a turning point. Unlike every other creature the Slyph had created, Grellnot existed only as a weapon, only as a force of destruction," Rivenwood answered him, the concern in his voice looming over every word.

"Grellnot is hunger, and that's all he is. But because he was born of the magic of two worlds, our world and the Slyph's Echo World, he always had the ... potential to be an even larger threat. Every time he took the power of a Bridgefinder, he grew. Now, he can take in the power of both our world and the Slyph's."

"With that power, he crossed the line from a large concern to a crisis. That was the reason the decision was made for one of us, one of the Shrouded, to make contact again with the Bridgefinders after all this time."

"Heather was chosen simply because she was powerful enough to take care of herself; street-smart, and tough enough to deal with anything we thought she might find on her mission. You were the target for several reasons; your dealings with the Elves made you known to us. We knew that you were a recent arrival to the Bridgefinders, and would be the most likely to listen to our concerns. The others still living would not be." Rivenwood finished his answer with what to Cendan experienced as a sigh.

"So, what now? Why bring me here? Why tell me all of this? What was the point?" Cendan queried Rivenwood. "Bringing me here wasn't necessary to warn us about Grellnot."

Rivenwood was silent for a long time before finally answering.

"No. It wasn't. Truthfully, this was not part of the plan. Heather's original plan was just for her to warn you all and then leave. But the chance to see the inside of the legendary Bridgefinders building, to see the fabled map in person, changed things for her."

"Then you got kicked out by Marcus, and we didn't know what to do. Did we leave you as a target for Grellnot? I do not know if his former inability to do anything to you still holds true; he has grown in power and ability a great deal since the last time he tried. Heather, in communication with the Elders of the Shrouded, decided to bring you here, for both your safety and at least, somewhat, our curiosity."

Rivenwood continued, "But you are here now, and we are unsure what else we should do with you."

Cendan pounced on the thought that had flickered around the edges of his mind since learning about this place and these people.

"Teach me. Just teach me. The Bridgefinders know nothing of magic anymore, and while I may find a book or journal about it, being taught to harness whatever it is I can do is a tool that I need, I must, have."

"We have considered this. We are, however, somewhat split on the idea. Teaching a Bridgefinder the ways of the Shrouded is something we weren't prepared to process; at least not yet. While I, being the most senior of the Elders am for the most part for this idea, some of the other Elders, who were born after the split between the two groups, are less than enthused about it. There is a faction who want to let Grellnot finish you all off, then find a way to defeat him. Ridding ourselves of both problems at once." Rivenwood responded.

"Problem? The Bridgefinders are a problem? Oh, you mean the Bridges being turned and forced to come near EVA? The closing of the Bridges and banishing of the creatures that come through? Do you really hate us that much to let us die?" Cendan was somewhat surprised by this. His mental image of the Shrouded was one of nature-magic-hippy-types being peaceful and hiding away from the real world. The idea that they would let the Bridgefinders be destroyed and killed by Grellnot, simply to get their way, pointed to a far darker turn of mind.

"Hate is a strong term for it, Cendan Key. Call it more like 'tough love'. There are those among us who feel that the Bridgefinders have brought this on themselves. That we shouldn't step in and save a group of people who proclaimed themselves the true protectors of the world and walked away from the Shrouded. I do not share this viewpoint, but it does exist. But that's immaterial for now. We have agreed as a whole to train you. To help you expand your powers and abilities in the short time we have left to do so." Rivenwood's voice softened. "We do not know how long it will take, but everything we can detect and find out says that Grellnot is plotting to strike at the Slyph. When he does so, the odds are high that he will win. We must be ready for that chance."

Cendan knew Rivenwood was right. The idea of Grellnot flush with all the power of the Slyph on top of all the power he already had was one that no one liked the idea of. It was obvious the Shrouded had mixed feelings about him being here, just as many in fact as what he had about being here. But they knew magic. They knew it far better than anything he could get out of books in the Maker library. It was different magic than Bridgefinder magic though he wasn't sure to what degree.

"Ok, let's do it then." Cendan answered quickly. "If only because the idea of a thing like Grellnot not being stopped is one that we can all agree is bad. Bad as they say with a capital 'B'."

Cendan broke contact with the tree Rivenwood, blinking in the light. Momentarily fuzzy headed, he struggled a bit to clear his mind. He wasn't even sure how long it had been since he started that conversation with Rivenwood. It was rather like waking up from a nap in the afternoon and not knowing how long you'd been asleep.

Heather was still there, though she was sitting now, her back to another nearby tree. Her eyes locked onto him with intensity.

"So, I have to train you now? Joy." She took her fetish off her wrist and spun the loop in a circle off her finger. "I'm to show you the basics, like tapping into the surrounding power. Using that power, your will, and your fetish to make things happen."

"You? They can't give me someone else?" Cendan blurted out. He still wasn't sure how he felt about Heather. If last night hadn't happened, he would have jumped at the chance to spend more time with her. But now? He didn't trust her. Maybe. He hated things like this. Emotions always got in the way of good solid logic and facts. Factually, he knew she was probably the best choice. She knew him, and if what Rivenwood had said was correct, the Shrouded probably didn't want a lot of interactions with him. It made sense for the one person who already had contact to continue it. He persisted nonetheless.

"I mean, what about a Creator? One of your Maker types," Cendan continued, seeing the look of anger and – what was that? Sadness maybe? – that crossed Heather's face at his first question. Her face set into a blank look, and Heather stood.

"Yes, after I show you the basics, you will get some time with a Creator." Without another word, Heather motioned him to follow her away from Rivenwood.

"Heather, I am sorry, but after last night I just…" Cendan trailed off, once again unsure how to deal with someone else's emotions.

"It's fine, Cendan. I shouldn't have done it in retrospect. I just didn't see what the big deal was for you. But I guess you see those sort of things very differently than I." Heather answered back, but didn't look at him. He knew that her feelings were hurt though he wasn't understanding why. She had been the one in the wrong, so why was she upset that he didn't want much to do with her. Emotions; so damn inconvenient when a decision needed to be made.

Chapter 14

They walked on in silence as Cendan took in the surrounding forest. It seemed a nice quiet place, though every now and then he'd remind himself that each tree he passed held the soul and mind of a departed Elder of the Shrouded, and he'd get creeped out a bit. His mind would, as they walked, wonder if that tree hated him, or had that trees branches moved against the breeze a bit? As they approached a clearing, he could feel his tension rising, and it was somewhat a relief to walk out of the trees.

Heather turned to face him, still somewhat unexpressive.

"This will do to learn some basics. This is going to be a crash course, Cendan. The Elders don't know how long we have until Grellnot makes its move on the Slyph. Because of that, I'm going to give you a rundown on the rules of magic, and how to shape it in a basic form. Normally this is taught to kids over several weeks. With you, I'm going to do it in an afternoon." A slight smile cracked her face, but to Cendan's mind, it wasn't a particularly pleasant one.

"Open yourself to your sight, Cendan, see the magic flowing around us. Do not turn back and look at the wood; not yet at any rate. But see the flow here in the clearing." Heather held up her fetish. "And get the thing you call a focus out of your pocket and into your hand."

Cendan sighed and grabbed the Key, welcoming the feel of the metal in his hand as he opened his mind up to see the magic.

The points of light that reflected the magic of his world were strong here, and for once not as randomly placed as he'd seen before. A pattern existed, more of one than he expected.

"What do you see, Cendan?" Heather asked.

"I see magic, but... they are laid out, organized," Cendan responded, his eyes locked on to the pattern. He knew patterns were important from what he had read in the Maker wing and trying to figure out systems was something he enjoyed long before any of this magic world stuff intruded into his life. Figuring this out took his mind off everything else, at least for a moment.

"Good. Yes, the magic here is structured a bit by the nature of its location, and what it's used for. This is a teaching field, so we keep the magic here a bit simpler to deal with."

Heather continued. "Look at my fetish, using your sight, what do you see?" Cendan looked up, but made sure he kept his eyes on her fetish, that twisted wooden hoop she held up high. The points of magic were circling it, flowing around it like tiny living ants, in a line, ordered.

"I can tell by your face you see the pattern. What I'm doing is charging my fetish. It's a simple basic skill. There are places in the world where the magic is weak, or places where it can be hard to force the magic to do what you want. Having a store of magic tied to your fetish can be a good thing. It allows you to have a well to tap into so you don't get caught unawares." Heather motioned Cendan to try. "You try. You call to the magic, form a mental image for it to follow. It's easy, though as you'll see…"

Cendan reached out to the magic, feeling it with his mind. At first he reached out strong, forcefully. The points seemed caught at first, but slid away from his mind. Almost like magnets repelling away from each other, the points didn't want to seem to go anywhere together.

"Not so easy is it?" Heather asked. "Magic doesn't like to be forced to do anything. This is the first lesson. You must be careful, but firm. A light touch will get you farther than a strong one, at least at first. You should get it though. You use magic in your scrying though you don't even know it. What you need to learn is how to do it consciously, and for more than one thing."

Cendan nodded. Again he reached out, and with less force, gently reached out and almost plucked the points up, one, and then another, until he had a rather large collection of points. But how to get them moving into his focus? Slowly, he placed the points into a pattern. It was difficult, the points reacted sort of like magnets repelling each other, but they also seemed as fragile and light as a soap bubble. It wasn't easy to get them to move in the way he wanted.

Sweat formed on his head as he could feel his face scrunch up a bit. How did Heather keep her face straight like that? This was hard. But slowly, the points fell in line. And to his surprise, once the pattern formed, it stayed and started flowing on its own.

"Very good, Cendan. Very. Normally that can take a week alone to get working for most students. And you've learned lesson two too: once a pattern starts, he naturally wants to keep moving that way. The hard part is getting it started."

"The pattern determines what happens. The key is learning how to get magic into that pattern and quickly. You can't stand around trying to concentrate and get everything setup if Grellnot is trying to eat you, literally," Heather added.

Cendan could see that she was attempting to put a happy face on the situation though his feelings about it all were still highly mixed.

"So is there a trick to that?" Cendan asked, keeping his attention on the lessons. "I mean, you do it fairly quickly from what I've seen."

Heather shrugged. "Not really. There are a few shortcuts, but the number one way is practice. Lots and lots of practice. Which takes time. Which you don't really have."

Cendan could feel the sigh rising up and squelched it. Practice always takes time.

"Shortcuts? Anything would be helpful."

"Once you've got a pattern down, you can store it in your fetish. I assume it would work the same way for yours, but then again, to me your Key feels... wrong."

Cendan started at that. This was the first time she had mentioned it since they met.

"What do you mean wrong?" His key felt right to him. In fact, since he'd been holding it, he realized his stress levels were down; way down.

"It's just so... cold. Hard. I can see the magic flowing through it, but its mechanical. Can you see the difference?"

Cendan looked at her fetish, and then at his key. In truth, she was onto something, though neither felt wrong to him. The magic flowed and moved in an almost organic living way on her fetish. In contrast, his followed the same pattern every time. His moved faster, but kept the same path. Odd, he thought. But more detail on the natural versus manmade split between the Bridgefinders and the Shrouded.

"I can, but yours doesn't feel wrong to me. Maybe inefficient, but not wrong," he answered without thinking. Inefficient? Think before you say things, Cendan, he berated himself.

Heather didn't answer, but her face once again went blank.

"Storing a pattern in the object in your hand isn't hard. And you still have to gather the magic, but it makes starting the working a bit faster." Cendan nodded. He didn't remark on his passing comment. Better to let it go.

"But how do I store it? I mean, I understand the reasons, and idea sounds understandable, but how?" Cendan asked.

Holding her fetish forward, Heather instructed him.

"You have the pattern for charging right? You need to take that pattern and force it into the fetish. Right now, it's on the outside. You must push it inside. Just for a moment. The object will, for the lack of a better term, save the pattern."

Cendan nodded. Sort of like how Oakheart had saved his memories and information onto the key, patterns of magic could be saved as-well. That made sense. Taking a breath, Cendan firmly but carefully pushed the pattern into the key. The points of light felt slippery still to him, and he found himself working hard to keep the pattern together. But slowly, it finally sunk into the key, just for a moment. He released his mental hold, and the pattern sprung back to the surface as if he'd never touched it.

"Good. Very good," Heather said out loud watching him. "You truly are gifted, Cendan. Now to access a pattern you have saved. First, we need to cancel the current pattern. This is lesson three. All magic, unless it's the permanent kind, needs to be unraveled when you're done. There are several reasons for this. One, it's very hard for another user of magic to unravel a pattern they didn't create. Doable, but not easy. The more complicated the pattern, the harder it is for someone else to undo."

"Also, leaving magic doing something, making it permanent, has a price. Part of you becomes the spell. That part never comes back unless somehow the permanence is undone. The more of you that becomes part of the magic, the less there is that is you. Until you can no longer be considered a person; your mind will be gone. Here in the Rivenwood, the permanent spells are actually few. The binding of an Elder to a tree is one of the exceptions. That spell sacrifices the body to save the mind." Heather pointed behind him. "Look now."

Cendan turned to look at the woods and caught his breath. The woods were alive in a pattern of lights. Thick and close, the pattern was a detailed as it was stunningly beautiful. The flow alone, the movement; the only word Cendan could place to it was a dance. A crazy, beautiful dance of light. Of pure magic. His logic and detachment failed him at the sight. How could they have created that?

"That pattern, that working you see, Cendan Key, is the work of both the Elder who is being bound into their tree, and a creator. I said making something permanent takes something away from you, remember. Creators, like you, have slightly different rules. You still need to learn the unraveling, but for you, knowing what a creator is capable of is important." Heather's voice came to him as he watched the pattern.

Cendan nodded absently, still trying to absorb the pattern he was seeing. The more he looked at it, the more it made sense to him, though it was still a breath-stopping sight.

"Cendan, pay attention." Heather's voice once again came from behind him. Reluctantly, he turned away from the forest to face her.

"That was incredible. I need to understand that; I need to know," Cendan said out loud. "Let me talk to a creator or Maker, or whatever you want to call it."

"In time!" Heather responded, holding up a hand to stop his protest. "First, you must learn how to unravel. This is too important to not teach you."

Holding up her fetish again, he could see the same flow as before, still interesting to look at, though nothing compared to the masterpiece behind him.

"Every spell, every working, has a soft point. Finding this point allows you to unravel the pattern. Feel the pattern on your key, Cendan. Each point. There will be one that feels different in your mind. It's a subtle difference. While the magic can be elusive, slippery in your mind, the one point will feel almost as if it's wrapped in something. Not slippery, but soft. For me, I always think that it feels like it's wrapped in a cotton ball."

Cendan concentrated. "Does it look any different? I'm not feeling…" There. That one green light, it didn't slip away like the others.

"No, it looks the same, but it just feels different. It's hard to describe," Heather answered.

"I think I may have found it," Cendan replied. "Maybe."

Heather nodded. "Here's another important point. Unless it's a permanent spell, one user of magic, be they Shrouded or Bridgefinder, cannot unravel someone else's spell."

Cendan frowned a bit at that. "Why should that make a difference?"

"I was always told because the pattern was tied to the creator. Only a permanent spell is tied to an object, not a person. Spells tied to a person can't be permanent." Heather held up a finger. "Now, you in your mind, reach for that soft light, and grab it, and remove it from the pattern. Like this."

With no other sign, Cendan saw the lights that denote the magic of the world fall away like water, leaving the fetish in her hand uncovered.

"There's still magic here, but now it's inside the fetish. But the spell to recharge that well is gone."

Heather motioned for Cendan to try. Cendan reached out, but the soft spot was hard to find again. He'd get a flash of it, but then it would be gone. Teeth gritted, Cendan furrowed his brow in concentration.

"Relax Cendan. You're trying to force it. Remember the touch, the first lesson. The same thing holds true for unraveling the spell. Forcing anything just makes it harder."

A long stream of breath later, Cendan nodded and tried again. This light touch stuff wasn't easy, he thought to himself. He wondered if there was a better way, one that would come easier to him. This wasn't the time to experiment, though, he reminded himself. There! That point was it. Lightly, he drew his concentration to that point and pulled.

The pattern fell apart, the points of light showering down to join the pattern on the ground. In moments, there was no sign he'd even cast a spell. A grin broke over his face. Casting a spell! Marcus would blow a gasket over that if he knew, not that he hadn't already. Jasmine wouldn't know what to do. Sal would have cheered up a storm, sadly. He felt a slight wave of regret pass over him. He hadn't known Sal well, but still, it would have been a help and nice to have someone else in the Bridgefinders, who would actually listen to him.

"Now... Practice." Heather paced around the clearing. "The three basics need to become second nature to you. Practice takes time. Something that is running out."

Heather looked around. The shadows had gained some length around them, but there was plenty of daylight left.

"This is what I think we should do. You stay here, in this clearing, and I'll go and see if I can find a Grower to talk to you. You stay here and practice. This area is set up for new students to practice on, so you can't really harm yourself, or anything else around here. Within reason." Heather paused. She looked at him with a sad expression, but said nothing and walked off.

Cendan wondered if she had wanted to talk about last night again. Maybe not. Setting that series of thoughts aside, Cendan turned his concentration to practice. A quick glance around the clearing showed him that he was alone, at least as far as walking around people were concerned. A deep breath, and Cendan willed himself to relax. If he truly used magic every time he did his mental exercise of the branches, then he could do this without thinking too hard about it.

Touching something with his mind, without touching it with his mind but knowing about it, was not something that came easy, Cendan decided rather fast. He half imagined it like one of those 'if a tree falls in the forest, does it make a sound?' things. He could feel them, but the moment he paid attention, they would slip away; almost oil like. He tried again, remembering the specks of light, the raw magic. Five tries in, finally the magic moved into a pattern for him. A simple pattern, but a pattern. He wanted the magic to make a light, a visible, simple light. The pattern they sprung into, once he had control of them, was once again a far more orderly and straightforward one than the one Heather had made.

Chalking the difference up to the known differences between the Shrouded and the Bridgefinders, Cendan practiced 'saving' the pattern in his focus. A light could always be a useful thing to have whenever he needed it. And normally, a light would be a pretty safe thing to do. He set the pattern to flow through his Key, watching it move in orderly motion around the metal and through it. Heather hadn't really said how long a pattern needed to be set on his focus before it got saved to it, but he figured a few minutes later, after watching the pattern repeat itself ten or more times, that things were good.

With another soft touch, he searched for and found the point of magic to pull out of the pattern. That was in fact getting easier to do. It occurred to Cendan he'd never had to unravel his pattern-thinking; the skill that Heather said was a form of scrying. He made a note to ask about it. Maybe he was unconsciously doing it just as he was unconsciously forming the pattern?

Looking around and seeing no one nearby, Cendan decided to try to retrieve a pattern from the key. Heather hadn't actually told him how to do this, but he wanted to push himself. He once again made contact with the magic, and this time fed it into the key with no pattern in mind, other than to make light. Nothing happened. Frowning, Cendan released the magic and searched through the key with his mind, looking for the light pattern he had just 'saved' to it.

Eyes widened and breath stopped at what he found. The Key was full of patterns. Patterns of great complexity; patterns that he wasn't sure what they were. He found his rather simple pattern, alongside works of art. Oakheart. This must be part of what Oakheart transferred to the key! Cendan couldn't believe his luck. It was a treasure trove of knowledge, one that Cendan had not expected.

Heather. He had to find Heather. He needed to know how to access patterns on his key. He started off in the direction she had headed, but stopped after a few steps. Heather had told him to stay here. She'd been pretty adamant about it. The other issue, of course, was that he wasn't sure he wanted Heather to know about all the patterns on the key. The trust level between them wasn't high, and that level of knowledge…

He also wasn't sure if he wanted the Shrouded to know as a whole. The information that Rivenwood had shared, that there were some here who didn't care if Grellnot wiped out the Bridgefinders, had been an eye opener. Did he want people or tree people to know about the patterns? Could they somehow take them if they knew? Trust. He didn't trust anyone, really; only himself. He didn't trust Marcus, he didn't trust Rivenwood, and he didn't trust Heather. The closest he got to trust was Jasmine, and he wasn't sure even about her sometimes. Her loyalty to what she thought the Bridgefinders were, had been strong.

Cendan decided to keep it to himself, for now. Just the light and the recharge patterns were the only ones he'd talk about, until he could get a chance to practice away from the Shrouded; away from any other prying, interested eyes. He did continue to practice getting control of the magic, forming a pattern, and releasing it again. He soon found his mind wandering, however, before realizing with a start that he was performing the actions without thinking!

"See I knew you could do it." Heather's voice came from behind him. "You just had to learn to do something you already did."

Cendan turned to see her alongside a non-descript woman in a brown and grey robe watching him.

"I see you decided to make a light spell. Practical," Heather noted.

"Yeah, but I can't figure out how to use the pattern for it in my Key. The pattern is there, but how to use it..." Cendan finished with a shrug.

"Ah yes. The order on things like that are a bit different. First you find the pattern in your fetish, then you draw the magic to it. It will flow into the pattern on its own. Patterns are better used for really complicated spells, however. Simple ones, it isn't really needed for." Heather motioned to the woman by her side. "This is Gardener Xid. She's willing to talk to you about how your abilities are different than others who can use magic."

Chapter 15

Gardener Xid gave Cendan an appraising look.

"I never thought I'd meet a Bridgefinder, and certainly not a... Maker. A Maker, right?"

Cendan nodded. The woman reminded him of a teacher he had years ago in primary school.

"Yes. I've not really made anything, though. All I have is notes and journals. Long on theory, very short on specifics."

Gardener Xid smirked a bit at that.

"Based on what I know, or at least have bene taught, I should say that doesn't surprise me." The Gardener turned to Heather and motioned her off. "Leave us now. This is not a subject of conversation for non-creators."

Heather's face had a ghost of an annoyance, but she nodded and walked away, towards the woods.

"Non-Gardeners always want to know how we do what we do. They wouldn't understand it, and couldn't succeed if they tried. But they might do something stupid, so we don't let them watch." The Gardener turned and walked away, down the path that Heather had originally left down when she had gone to find her. "Come on Bridgefinder!" she yelled without looking behind her.

Cendan paused and then followed. It wasn't like he had much choice. Staying wouldn't get him anywhere.

"I'm going to take you to where I work. Where I grow things. I'm not sure how things will be different for you, being as you're not one of the Shrouded, but hopefully this will fill in some gaps." The Gardener walked quickly, efficiently. Cendan kept up, but kept looking around. He had never closed off his sight, and could see all the surrounding patterns, and was very unclear on what any of them did. The Gardener disturbed his thoughts.

"I do ask for something in return. I'd like to see your fetish. No sorry, Bridgefinders call them... a focus, right?" Xid shook her head. "Gardeners learn about our cousins more than most, but it's been a long time since I was taught any of that."

Cendan paused. "I don't know... This Key is very important to me." His grip on the key tightened.

"I don't mean it any harm. And I won't try to access the key; I simply want to examine its construction. It will be a learning exercise for us both."

Cendan still felt unsure, but the Gardener didn't wait for him as she continued to walk. Jogging to catch up, he decided to try to be social.

"My name is Cendan, by the way. Cendan Key. Pun not intended," he said, as he waved his focus a bit in his hand. "Heather said you were Gardener Xid, right? How many Gardeners are there?"

"Three," came the reply, with no other information. Cendan waited for some other acknowledgement, but no other words escaped her. Finally, he could see a low door ahead, cut into the hillside. He stopped mid stride, however, at what his magic sight showed him. The pattern, the magic, was different here. Very different. There was, to his mind, what appeared to be a fountain of magic literally spurting the lights into the air as they flowed.

Just as when Heather worked the stuff, this seemed organic, grown. A pattern of intricate beauty, one that seemed to flow with the earth itself.

"This is a special place. It's why I chose to work here. A place where magic, the raw magic of our world, is created. There are layers upon layers of subtle workings here, subtle calls and patterns. Generations of Gardeners have worked to create this place."

Cendan nodded; he could believe it. Gardener Xid came to the door and took something – Cendan couldn't make out what – and moved it rapidly across the door in a pattern. The door opened without a sound. The Gardener stepped through and motioned Cendan to follow her.

The room they walked into was the first somewhat familiar thing he'd seen today. It was a work room. Tools lined the walls, all hand tools, but they were recognizable. In fact, the room gave him the feeling of purpose and creation in a way he was somewhat surprised by. A low laugh came from Xid.

"If I had any doubts you were a Maker, it's gone now. The look on your face as we walked in gave it away. Only those with the talent react the way you did."

The Gardener looked Cendan up and down, examining him as one would examine a block of wood, or clay. Cendan got the distinct impression she was sizing him up to see what she could do with him.

"Cendan, right? Cendan, I will tell you a few things, show you more. But just like what you practiced with our young chosen diplomat to the Bridgefinders, Heather, the best thing is practice; lots and lots of practice." Grabbing a stool under the workbench, Xid sat. Cendan followed her lead and sat facing her.

"Now. I understand Heather told you the three main lessons of working magic. How to hold it, making a pattern and how to release it, and why. She even told you about making a pattern permanent, yes?" Cendan nodded. "Good. Now, what Heather doesn't know, and anyone with the talent for creating does know, is that all of that carries a big fat asterisk." Xid held up a pendant that she wore around her neck. An intricate knotted work pattern covered it and formed tiny cages where even small wood balls floated around. "This is my fetish. I grew this myself. Here, in the workshop."

"I'm sure you all, you Makers, do things differently. I can't help you with that. But I can cover what I think are similarities. Now, you have the sight open, yes?" Cendan nodded. "Good. Now, what do you see when you look at my fetish?"

Cendan peered at the pendant, now seeing anything other than the wood itself. He looked harder.

"No, it just looks like wood to me." Cendan paused. "You know, that doesn't make sense. We have these foci, or fetish, or whatever you call it. We work magic with it. You can imprint magic on it. You can even store magic in it. But yet, on the sight, you see nothing."

The Gardener smiled. "Exactly. What Heather doesn't know is that there are two kinds of sight. One all users of the magic can use, and one that only those with the talent for creation can use. You can do this. Keep your sight open, but with the same light touch you use to take the magic up before forming a pattern, I want you to take the un-patterned magic and flow it through your sight."

Cendan cocked at that. "I thought all magic needed a pattern?"

Xid just smiled. "For someone without the talent, that's true. Just try, Cendan Key. Just try."

Letting out a long breath, Cendan looked at the fetish with the sight and tried to follow the directions. He fumbled with the magic a few times in his attempt to have it flow through his sight. Then, on the fourth try, it worked.

The Pendant lit up like a rainbow in front of him. Bright colors, near gem-like clarity, enveloped the pendant. It in no way resembled wood anymore.

"That is amazing!" Cendan burst out. Holding onto his new sight, he looked at his own focus. The thing was covered with grooves with the new way of looking. Each groove held magic, moving like electricity, but the colors were as vibrant and strong as the pendant had been. And oddly enough, the parts that didn't have light on them were dark, nearly black. But even there, he could see... something. Even smaller channels, maybe? And even smaller lights? He found himself wishing for a microscope to look at it with.

"Yes. Your... focus you called it? Your focus is very different from our work. But based on what I'm seeing, just as powerful. But let's continue."

Gardener Xid pointed to her pendant. Now, what you're seeing is the combination of both the pendant itself, and the magic stored in it. If I were to discharge the well, it would still glow in your sight, but far less. I imagine the same holds true for your Key. Xid held up her hand with two fingers held up.

"Call these supplemental rules for those with the talent. One: any pattern can be tied to an item wrought with the magic. Once it's tied, its permanent to all but another with the talent. Two: to unravel another's work is very, very hard, and carries great risk." Xid pointed to Cendan's key again. "That was Oakheart's focus. He created after he left us and joined the Bridgefinders, right? That gives you some level of protection from the possible harm if you ever unraveled a bound-magic created by Oakheart."

"Normally, if I tried to unravel something you created, something bound, I'd have to be very careful. One wrong step, and I could lose my power forever. I could die, I could kill someone else depending on what the item was and what it could do." Xid looked at Cendan with a decidedly serious expression.

"My teacher told me once, years ago, a Gardener created a gate. A gate that formed a Bridge to the Echo world. A permanent gate. The Gardener in question made it for a nymph – yes, a classical nymph and all that the name implies. And it worked; the nymph could use it to come here, and by the virtue of him having the talent, he could visit her. But another Gardener saw the nymph, and as is the way sometimes, was overcome by lust for her. He couldn't bear the thought of seeing them together."

"He decided to unravel the gate with the other Gardener on one side, and the nymph on the other. But during the unraveling, something went wrong. The gate ripped a hole into... Well, we don't know where. But the Gardener who was doing the unraveling, was dragged into the gate just for a second and vanished. Just as quickly, he was thrown back out, but what came back was... not normal. He was smoking, and held his hands to his head, screaming. Screaming about whatever it was he had seen. The gate was destroyed, and sadly the nymph was too, as the gate exploded on the other side as-well."

Cendan nodded. "But... how can you all know this? If someone saw him why didn't they stop him?"

Xid smiled, a thin lipped one this time. "In time, some sort of sanity returned; enough to get the story at least out of him. He was never the same though." Xid paused then locked eyes with Cendan. "He was also my brother." Cendan paused and nodded.

"As I said, that key will give you some protection as it is part of Oakheart's... profile, I'll call it. And I don't think you will need to use it to do so, honestly. But seeing as how Oakheart was the last one with the talent who was also a Bridgefinder, I thought it worth mentioning."

Cendan nodded.

"Ok, now: how to tie things to an object." Xid handed him a small wooden ball. "We are going to make this light up, without you needing to cast the spell at all. First, you need to charge it. Similar to how your fetish – sorry focus; I'll get that right sometime – is charged. Cram it full of magic."

Cendan did so. It was hard however; the ball wasn't a repository for magic normally, and it didn't want to stick like it did with his focus.

"Not bad. It's harder than you think though, isn't it? Okay, so it's full. Now keep it that way. At the same time, pull more magic and form the pattern for the light spell."

Cendan found this to be harder still. With one part of his mind trying to keep the lights of the magic from spilling out of something they didn't want to be in, and the other grabbing magic and forming the right pattern, he could feel the sweat forming on him, even though it was cool in this workroom.

Finally, he thought he had it.

"Ok... I think." Xid seemed to examine the ball and gave him a small smile.

"Ok, now you're going to overlay the pattern on the ball, but instead of having it flow over the ball and off, you are going to tie it to the magic stored inside the ball. There won't be a start and an end, but a loop. A loop that pulls from itself."

Nodding, he tried to make it happen. The lights kept wanting to slip away, and the pattern didn't want to loop.

"Careful." Xid admonished him. "It's not easy, but you're doing well."

Cendan concentrated again. Suddenly he felt a click, and the pattern stabilized on the ball.

"Great job!" Xid exclaimed. Cendan looked at the ball with his new sight and liked what he saw. The stable pattern was there; the magic was there. But how to make it light?

"Gardener Xid. I see it all, but it doesn't glow?"

Xid laughed. "Will it to. Just like you will a Bridge to close."

Cendan shrugged and did so. Light bloomed, bright and strong, giving everything a slightly harsh look in the bright while light.

"Turn it down a bit, would you?" Xid laughed.

Cendan felt a little sheepish and did so. Now a nice soft glow was in the palm of his hand.

"How long will it last?" Cendan asked, studying it.

"Functionally forever. Barring the total destruction of the planet, the end of magic, or the merging of our world with the Slyph's echo," Xid answered. "You have done very well. Now, practice.

Lots of practice. Through the door behind me, there are rooms for sleeping, eating, bathrooms, and two smaller workrooms. Both were set up years ago for students. For whatever time we have left until either the Slyph or Grellnot wins, you can stay here and practice, practice, practice."

Cendan nodded. "Can I go and check it out?"

Xid smiled. "Of course. Feel free. I'll get a few things together for food. I'm sure Heather didn't feed you much." At the thought of food, Cendan felt his stomach rumble.

"No, actually. Haven't eaten since breakfast."

Xid nodded, shooing him through the door.

"Go on then, I'll get it organized." Cendan headed off the hall and Xid's face took on a decidedly darker cast. "He's far too powerful to let run around free. I'll have to let the Elders know."

Chapter 16

Marcus grimaced again, looking at the unconscious form of Jasmine laying on the table in one of the old creature study rooms. Why could she not see how much Cendan had destroyed their world? Why did she not understand? And then she had brought a witch, one of those outside the Bridgefinders who frolicked and did who knows what with the creatures of the Slyph. And she brought one into here, into this place; the seat of the Bridgefinders power.

Marcus had nearly screamed with rage when he had found out. With the stone sphere in his hand, he had felt a momentary compulsion to kill Jasmine. Smash her head in, his mind demanded, end the life of any betrayers! He hadn't, but it had been a struggle not to. His head hurt so much these days, and he was tired, so very tired. He couldn't remember when he'd last really slept, when he'd actually really eaten, or even taken a shower.

He spent all his time either questioning Jasmine over and over again, searching for some reason to trust her again, or sitting in the dark, reaching out through the sphere into the headquarters; finding out what the sphere could do. He was never without it now. It stayed in his hand, even when he would finally collapse into short restless naps. He knew it better than his own focus, which, though he still wore it, he'd not touched with that part of his mind in days; weeks even.

He remembered the day he'd gotten the sphere. Two days after Sal's death, before he had realized the depths of Cendan's true evil nature. He'd gone to the Maker wing on his own, unable to sleep. He'd been reading about the construction of the headquarters, and how it had been done. Then he'd seen the reference. The reference to the Keystone.

Just a hint, but it looked interesting. He'd looked for more and found that the Keystone was only able to be used by the leader of the Bridgefinders. Marcus had been proud then. Finally, being the leader meant something. He'd always been somewhat ashamed of the fact that being the leader really meant nothing when there were only three of them. And when Cendan had joined, it had been even less; a Maker was far more important than he was. Jasmine and Sal had practically fawned over Cendan when they had found out.

But this, the Keystone; that would elevate him, at least according to the notes he had read. He knew what it looked like as-well, thanks to some long ago Bridgefinders notes. He had searched in secret for three days before he found it. Locked in a chest up on a shelf in the Maker wing. As soon as he had grasped it, the connection between himself at the headquarters had blossomed in his mind.

The others were giving him space to mourn Sal, he knew, which meant he had time to explore. And the more he used the sphere, the more he understood. Cendan was the problem; he had to go. But how? The days and nights ran together as he had sat in the barrier room, examining the sphere, reaching out with it. It was only then he knew; Cendan was not only the problem, EVA was as-well. It was so clear now.

Then Cendan had come to him, logical and superior, just because he was a Maker. Cendan wasn't the leader of the Bridgefinders. He was! Cendan didn't get to call the shots; he did! But how to get rid of him was elusive until the Map. Cendan had broken it, Marcus was sure of it. Broken it and blamed the Slyph. Dragged Jasmine into his evil by somehow tricking her into bringing a witch into this place. Plating a creature of the Slyph even, to draw attention away from himself, the true villain.

With the sphere, he had cut EVA and Cendan off from one another. He'd also been able to banish Cendan from the place. It had been hard, but with his new power he could reach new heights, and go down as the most powerful Bridgefinder who ever lived. He daydreamed sometimes about future generations of Bridgefinders, learning about the great Marcus Wheeldon. Cendan would be a footnote.

He reached out again with the Sphere, towards Jasmine's unconscious form. She was still out, in some form of heavy sleep that he didn't quite understand. It wasn't magic, Marcus knew; it couldn't be. It was some extension of their inborn abilities. It had kept her under for days now, without need for food or water.

She was so beautiful lying there. Marcus felt the old pain in his chest. He loved her. It was the only reason he hadn't killed her that day when the rage and anger at her betrayal had come. He had loved her since they were children. Why didn't she understand? They were meant for each other! A slew of special full blooded Bridgefinder children was supposed to be their future. Ten or more! They could have brought the Bridgefinders back from the edge of destruction.

But she didn't want him. She didn't love him. She had even dated Cendan, throwing that in his face when they had first met the stupid Maker. She should have been his! Marcus, the leader of the Bridgefinders, should get what he wants, and that was Jasmine. His tongue licked his lips as his gaze wandered over her unconscious form. Maybe later... Marcus shook his head. Why did his head hurt so much these days?

Wheeling around, Marcus stalked down the hall away from Jasmine. She would be fine there, for now. And if somehow she woke up, the restraints would keep her locked down until Marcus came back. Maybe the headaches had something to do with the Sphere, he wondered. Marcus changed direction and headed toward the Maker wing, the only place he'd find anything about his symbol of authority.

The Maker wing was open as always now, and even in his delirious state, he felt a bit of a thrill at crossing that door. Cendan's only good deed. Not that the fool deserved even that credit. If the old Bridgefinders hadn't stored the Keystone here, there would have been knowledge to share for years. The Keystone could unlock any door in the place.

Setting himself down in the primary study, Marcus began searching though the books and journals, searching for more information on the sphere. Some notes about foci and the sphere turned up in the first book, but he didn't understand it. Resonance? Uncontrollable fluctuations? Marcus tossed the book off to the side. Idiots. He was in complete control of the sphere. He was the singular power here, and he was in control!

Grabbing another journal off the stack that Cendan had left before his departure, Marcus noted the symbol of the Maker known as Oakheart on the cover. This was all partially his fault too, Marcus felt. If Oakheart had not been captured, things would have been different.

"Makers are dangerous, powerful fools," Marcus said out loud to the silence and gloom. A wave of pain and nausea interrupted his reading, and he nearly doubled over.

Maybe what was happening to him was something Cendan had done. Revenge of sorts, for Marcus asserting his right as leader to banish him. Yes. That made sense; of course that was it. Hatred for Cendan burned brighter still. Cendan had first nearly destroyed the Bridgefinders and now was striking back at him somehow. Bitter bile filled Marcus as he thought of the Maker dating his love, destroying the one thing that Marcus honored above all. He hated him. He hated him so much.

To calm himself, Marcus started flipping through the journal of Oakheart's. At least Oakheart had illustrated most of his notes. Most of it didn't make sense to him; Maker gibberish he thought. The last third of the book was in fact blank. It must have been a late one, even possibly the last one before the fool got captured. He was about to toss it and reach for a new journal when the sphere in his hand seemed to writhe as it got close to the book.

Marcus stopped mid-throw. He slowly brought them together, feeling the sphere seem to move in his hand once more. Words formed on the blank pages, new words, clear and plain. He spoke them to himself.

"Notes on the cutting of the bindings. The keyhole is in place. EVA is highly skeptical of the idea and actively argues against it. I too am unsure if we should ever use it. Cutting the binding between our world and the Slyph's will have unknown consequences. While the Slyph and her creatures would be hard pressed to ever form another Bridge to our world, I do not know what that would mean for the Spinner and Valkith's other children. Still, the unbinding exists as a failsafe. A method when all hope is lost to separate us from her. She comes to me sometimes as I sleep, saying she has plans for me. I hate those nights. My focus will be the only method of starting the unbinding; I do not trust anyone else with the responsibility. I will erase my memories of this. These notes will only appear when my focus is used, or in the presence of that thrice damned

Keystone. The keyhole is in EVA's main mechanism room, upper wall, hidden from normal view."

Marcus paused and read it again. A way of separating our world from the Slyph's? Forever? And the fool had never used it? Who was the Spinner? Valkith? What was that? Marcus rubbed his forehead. The pain was back up, in force. It didn't matter who they were. The only thing that mattered was that there was a way to end the threat of the Slyph forever. Once again, a Maker had placed himself above the rest of the Bridgefinders. They shouldn't be allowed to run free. Makers should be kept here, locked up safe and away from any decisions. Doing the one thing they were good for, making things for the true Bridgefinders to use.

But it needed Oakheart's focus, which was Cendan's focus. A groan escaped him. Cendan had the focus with him when he left. He had to find a way to get that focus. He had to find a way to get Cendan back here.

Chapter 17

Cendan stretched, his back grumbling at the hard mattress he'd been sleeping on now for three days. The room he'd been given here, in Gardener Xid's workshop, was sparse and somewhat primitive. A wry smile escaped him as he looked around. In truth, the place looked like a set from a medieval fantasy movie. The place didn't even really have running water; he had to use magic as an exercise to get any to fill the bowl on the counter. The bathrooms were even worse. Cendan shuddered a bit at that thought.

Still, the constant practice had given him far more than he'd otherwise get. Gathering magic, forming the pattern and unraveling the pattern when he was done was starting to become second nature. Xid had commented more than once in the last days that he was taking to this faster than she had ever thought possible. He personally chalked it up to what Heather had told him. His tree and branch thought exercise was actually him working magic. He'd been doing it for years.

Cendan took his focus and held it in his hand, delving that part of his mind into the stored patterns in the key. He'd been doing this every morning he'd been here. Trying to explore, catalog, and know these patterns. Some had made a lot of sense: he had the pattern for how to make a focus; how to tie something to the magic of this world; even how to tie things to the magic of the Bridgefinders headquarters that chunk of matter stuck between the two worlds.

More mundane things as well: pulling water; making wind; a basic sleep pattern. Patterns to strengthen iron and wood, and one to make cloth change colors for some odd reason. But the larger share of patterns were highly complex, and for those he didn't have a clue. He assumed that most of them were for larger projects involved in making. In at least one of them, he could see parts of other simpler patterns. There wasn't any place to practice any of them. While Xid had been helpful as a whole, his natural distrust of the Shrouded kept him from saying anything.

Xid had been somewhat dodgy in responses when asked about how long he'd be here, and even more vague when he asked about Heather. He'd not seen her since that first day, and that worried him, though he wasn't sure why. It's not like Heather was his friend; he still couldn't believe that she'd used magic to seduce him like that. It seemed distant, unreal when he thought about it. Cendan still was bothered by the fact that no one would tell him where she was though.

Working the water pattern and getting cleaned up helped him put that all out of his mind, for now at least. It was rolling around in a back corner somewhere in his head, but he forced himself to ignore it. He needed to get to the workroom, and he didn't want to be late. Today, Xid was going to start teaching him about Bridges. He had seen Heather form one once, but he'd not been as observant as he should have been at the time.

Getting dressed in some clothes they had provided him, simple clean linen garments, he made his way to the workroom. Gardener Xid was already there, and she was with Heather! A smile broke out on Cendan's face; that somewhat surprised even him.

"Heather! There you are."

Heather looked at him with a somewhat bemused expression.

"Was I lost? I do have other things to do than lead you around like a child, Cendan." The smile fell off Cendan's face. Why had he been smiling anyways?

"Why are you here today, then? Throwing more shaded insults at me?" he threw back at her.

Heather paused and shook her head. "Sorry, Cendan, it's not been a... good few days. And for you, it's going to get worse." Heather reached into a bag on the main workbench. "Remember when I met you? I told you two things that day. One was about the war between Grellnot and the Slyph. And rightfully, that is the main problem for all of us. But you, Cendan Key, still have another problem. One you're going to need to fix and fix soon."

Cendan frowned for a second. "Oh the Elves? Yeah, but I don't see why that's as big of a deal as everyone seems to think it is. The Elves are trapped on the Echo world, right? They can't do anything to me, and they can't come here. They're powerless."

The expressions on Heather and Xid's face, however, didn't seem to support this.

"No. They aren't," Heather replied. "I have to remember that you aren't one of us; you don't have a lot of experience dealing with the Echo world, or its creatures. Do you think it was chance the Elves found you? Just blind luck? They have been hunting for someone to get them around the Slyph's ban for a long time, Cendan. I imagine a few subtle weavings were done on you the moment they detected you, to get you to them."

"Weavings?" Cendan stopped her.

"Yeah, magic used on the Echo World is called a weaving. Not important, focus." Heather retorted. "Remember, while the Elves were banned by the Slyph from coming here, they command a great deal of power on their own world. They were made to be like us, to need us, in many ways they are only second to the Slyph herself in raw power. Do you understand?"

Cendan shrugged. "Ok, so the Elves are powerful, but they can't come here."

Rolling eyes from Heather greeted that statement, and she was about to retort when Xid stopped her.

"Cendan. We know that Grellnot and the Slyph are about to have a showdown. The Elves are the premier spell casters of the Echo World. If they strike a deal with Grellnot, do you know how powerful that will make him? If Grellnot agrees to end their banishment in exchange for their help, there isn't a place on the planet you could hide from them."

Cendan hadn't thought about it in that way and felt a wave of annoyance wash over him. He should have seen it.

"The Elves hate Grellnot, though," he answered back. "But…"

Xid nodded. "But to get back to Earth? To end their banishment? That bargain is one they would even make with Grellnot. But if you fulfill it first, they can't. They simply can't. It's hard wired into the Elves; once a bargain made is a bargain kept, the bargain can't be redone."

Cendan ran with it. "So if I fulfill my bargain, the Elves can't make a deal with Grellnot. And the only thing they would want is to end their banishment. But, say I make a new Bridge for them to use. Can't they still make a deal with Grellnot to fix the

Bridge in their settlement? The one I used to come home? It still works; they just can't use it."

"No. Not if you attach your Bridge end point to their Bridge," Heather answered. "And you are on short notice, Cendan. A Bridge formed elsewhere here in the Rivenwood. A Bridge that a Scowler came through and delivered this; for you."

Heather pulled a hood out of the bag that she'd had her hand in. A hood. A hood from one of the women in the Elven village. His stomach still lurched at the thought of those women.

"It's a message of sorts for you. Time is short." Heather threw the hood at him.

"You know what this is, Heather? Xid? You know what the Elves want?" Cendan held the hood with a sense of dread. "If I help them, they are going to take women from this world, and I... I don't know what they do to them but they use them to..."

Heather nodded. "I'm aware. Some may welcome that fate, who knows. But I know."

Xid, grim faced, added, "It was a foolish bargain to make, to agree to bring them back to this world, to take young women off to be used as nothing more than brood stock."

The air went out of Cendan then. It had been a foolish deal. He hadn't known what it meant. But a bargain was a bargain. He was going to consign an unknown number of women and girls to a fate that was beyond anything he'd ever thought of. Damn fool bargain. Bargain. An idle thought stirred.

"Wait..." Cendan found a bench and sat down. What had been the exact words of the bargain? He had promised to find them a way into this world. That was what they had wanted, what they still wanted.

A small smile broke across his face and grew.

"Quick, is there a fast way to travel using magic? I mean, say you wanted to go to Rome? Hawaii? Sweden? It doesn't matter, just is there a way to travel very fast?" Xid and Heather paused and exchanged glances.

"You can't run away from this, Cendan," Heather replied.

Xid added in, "Nor would we let you. You must fulfill your end of the bargain."

"No. You don't understand, just answer the question. I'm not running." Cendan was grinning widely now. "So, is there a way?"

Xid slowly nodded. "Yes, but it has drawbacks. And it's taxing; we don't use that pattern much." Heather had a somewhat surprised look and glanced at Xid.

"There is? I was never shown that."

Xid waved her off. "It's a Gardener thing. Non-creators can't even use the pattern."

Lips pursed, Heather looked at Xid with annoyance, but said nothing else. Cendan, still grinning, threw her a thumbs up.

"Ok. So teach me about Bridges. Then teach me the pattern for this travel thing. You can even come with me; I don't care."

Heather broke in. "What is going on in that head of yours? You're acting a little… out of sorts."

Cendan shrugged. "I think I've found a way to fix my Elven issue. Just like you all wanted. And me too for that matter."

Two hours later, Cendan had the basics of the pattern for Bridges down, including how to tie a Bridge to an existing Bridge on the Echo World. Heather and Xid once again remarked on how fast he was picking this up.

"It took me nearly a month to get Bridges down, Cendan, and you're doing this in hours," Heather said, the tone of annoyance back in her voice. "How can you be doing this so fast?"

Cendan just shrugged. "Patterns and systems come to me naturally. This is just another system."

Gardener Xid looked at Cendan and sighed. "I expect you want me to show you this travel thing now? It will exhaust you for nearly a day to travel that way, and to come back."

Cendan nodded, then paused. "Can you bring someone else with you? Like, could I take Heather somewhere?"

Laughter erupted from Heather at that.

"Want me to run away with you now, Cendan? First you get mad about me cutting out the mess of dating and wot-not with magic, and now you want me to run away with you?"

That faded Cendan's smile. "No. I need to know is all. I have no desire to run away with you, Heather. None. And I never will."

Heather's laugh slowly died out, and she looked away.

Xid sighed. "Children. Yes, but only if they have the creator knack. So you could take me, or I could take you." Cendan shifted his attention back to Xid.

"Ok so if I have you take me elsewhere; can you bring us both back here?"

The Gardener shifted from foot to foot. "Yes. But I'd be useless the next day." Cendan nodded and rubbed his face.

"Ok then. I have a plan. Based on what I promised Lachnin, based on the words of our bargain, I promised Lachnin that I would create a Bridge or item that allowed them to come back to our world. But I never said where. I never said it would be any place useful. I never said it would have people on it."

Cendan blurted out, "If I rejoin the Bridge that they have to a location out in the middle of nowhere, an atoll in the south pacific somewhere, I will have fulfilled my bargain."

A look of grudging respect came over Heather's face.

"That is actually a good plan." Gardener Xid nodded as well.

"You know that that won't totally stop them though, Cendan. The elves can work magic," Xid reminded him.

Cendan nodded. "I know. But can they work our magic? Meaning, the magic of our world?" Xid shook her head.

"No, they'd have to draw through the Bridge to weave anything."

Cendan nodded. "I hoped so. So they'd be out in the middle of nowhere, with little magic, but they'd still be here, and I will have bought time and potentially removed them from the equation in terms of Grellnot."

Heather shrugged. "It's a decent plan. Far better than doing nothing."

Gardener Xid nodded as well. "It buys us time. I don't like the idea of being exhausted tomorrow, but it gives you time, and by extension all of us."

Xid checked a clock on the wall.

"It's close to noon now. I need two hours to prepare. Can I meet you in the training field at two?"

Cendan nodded. "Heather, are you coming to see us off?"

Heather, who had been looking at Xid with an expression of confusion, glanced at Cendan with a smile

"Sure. Why not? If only to see this Gardener-only pattern."

Xid grunted as she stood. "See you at two then." Xid headed for the door leading outside. Heather watched her go and turned to Cendan.

"That's odd. Patterns don't require…" She trailed off. "Never mind, just… I'll see you at two." Heather turned and followed Xid out the door.

Cendan muttered, "People. Never make any damn sense." And with that, he returned to his room to practice more patterns. At least those made sense.

Gardener Xid approached the wood quickly. Turning through it, she headed towards a far corner. She paused in front of a hemlock tree, large and majestic.

"I can't commune, I'm being followed. The Bridgefinder is getting more powerful. If we are going to stop him, it needs to be soon."

At exactly two pm, Cendan, Heather and Gardener Xid met at the practice field. It had only been a few days since Cendan had been there last, but it seemed like a near eternity. He had learned so much, seen more of the power of magic than he had even imagined. Even in the few hours since he'd seen the other two, he'd figured out a new pattern in the stored ones in the Key, one that would allow him to mirror another pattern! As long as it was cast within minutes of that pattern.

He'd had fun with that, creating mirrors of mirrors with the lights he'd summoned in his little room in the workshop. The mirrors didn't last long; unlike a normal pattern these fell apart on their own fairly fast, but still, it was fun to play with. He'd also spent a few minutes before coming over finding an appropriate anchor for his plan. Bridges, permanent ones at least, needed to be anchored, according to Xid. He'd chosen a fairly heavy stone block. It wouldn't get blown away in the wind, or easily washed away; that was the hope at least. And if it did, well, the Elves' Bridge would open up into the ocean, and still he would fulfill his bargain.

He'd found a small atoll in the South Pacific Ocean. Small, uninhabited, not even a tree on it. A spit of sand and small brush. At least the nearly decade old book, an actual old school encyclopedia, had described it as such. At first he'd found the book amusing, but quickly realized this was needed in places like this. Magic didn't seem to mix super well with modern technology, or at least no one had tried, so things like actual encyclopedias were useful.

Heather stood off to one side, but uncharacteristically, looked somewhat concerned. Her eyes never left Xid, watching every move she made. Xid didn't notice though Cendan noticed the occasional twitch in her hands as she began to gather the surrounding magic.

"This isn't an easy pattern, Cendan. Please don't attempt this on your own," Xid remarked. She was right, Cendan could see.

The points of magic were flowing around her, folding in on themselves and her in a mind bending way.

"A tube?" Cendan asked out loud though he wasn't sure whom he was talking to.

"Sort of. In the most basic terms, the pattern folds the space between us and the destination in a very small localized area, and forms a tube for us to travel through," Xid answered through her teeth. The strain was obvious as sweat formed on her brow, even despite the cool air of Rivenwood. "Quickly, the destination."

Cendan nodded. "I have a set of coordinates…"

Xid cut him off. "Useless. Form the destination in your mind and grab my arm. But be clear in your thoughts!"

Cendan felt a thrill of fear race up his spine, but squelched it. Forming a picture of the atoll he'd found, he grabbed Xid's arm. The feeling of travel was very unlike the transitions he'd felt when going to the Echo World, or when he'd entered or left the Bridgefinders lair. This was on the edge of extreme pain, and it lasted far longer than the other transitions. He alternately felt like his skin was going to get worn off, or his hair would get ripped out. The wind that blew through the tunnel with them was more than intense and pushing against it forced him into some unusual contortions.

Chapter 18

Just as suddenly as it started, however, it ended. Bright warm light enveloped them as Cendan blinked a few times. The salt air greeted his sense of smell, just as the waves greeted his ears. They had, in all appearances, made it. Taking a moment to take it all in, Cendan could understand why that method of travel was rarely used. It was one of the more unpleasant things he'd ever done. Parts of his skin, the exposed parts at least, were still aching from the battering they'd received; and they still had to go back! Xid didn't seem to be much better; her eyes were still closed as she breathed in and out slowly.

"Xid? You ok?" Cendan asked. He'd liked to think they were becoming friends. She had taught him a lot, and while not warm per se, she was highly competent. A trait that, to Cendan, was far too underrated.

"Yes, just hadn't done that in quite some time. I had forgotten how intense that pattern can be," Xid answered. Her eyes cracked open a bit as she shaded her view with her hand. "Well it appears you held the image well. Nice place you picked," Xid said, as she looked around.

"Thanks. It's out in the middle of nowhere in the ocean. It's not even visited by research ships. The closest landmass is nearly a thousand miles from here. The Elves can come here and make sand castles for all I care. I will have fulfilled my end of the bargain, at any rate." Cendan took the heavy square stone out of his pocket. It wasn't especially large, the size of a small box, but it was far heavier than it looked.

"Next time, ask before you take something from the workshop, Cendan." Xid pointed at the stone. "I don't have a lot of that left. You can use it, but… next time ask."

Cendan nodded in assent and walked toward what was roughly the middle of this tiny sand island. No real animal life, other than feathers from birds, and what appeared to be a long dead sea-turtle shell. As he had hoped, pretty empty and barren. He made a small mound of sand and placed the soon to be anchor stone on top.

"Ok, so I'll connect the Bridge from here to the Elven village in the Echo. I assume they will know something is up, so they may head this way. I expect that they won't be terribly happy with this resolution, so we will need to leave fast. Are you ready to travel back? I mean, are you too tired? Do you need me to wait?"

"No. I'm fine. The way back is easier anyway, and before you ask, no I don't know why. It just is."

Cendan nodded and smiled at her response. Since he'd met her, he must have asked her why about thirty times a day on anything and everything she had taught him.

"Ok then, let's get this done," Cendan said squaring his shoulders. He took a deep breath and let it out slowly. This was, arguably, going to be the toughest pattern he'd ever attempted. He knew he could do it; he had to do it. There was no room for doubt here.

Opening himself up to the sight, the specks and points of light around him showed the magic overlaying everything. Less than in Rivenwood for sure, but enough for what he needed to do here. Reaching out, he started gathering the magic slowly and carefully. Specks became points, which became blobs of magic, rainbow colored and flashing in his magic sight.

"Good; careful and slow," Xid commented from beside him, watching him work. Finally, after far more time than he thought it should take, he felt like he had enough to work the pattern.

Reaching out, he began to form the pattern for the Bridge, open ended for now, but still the pattern. As more and more points fell into it, the spiral of the Bridge formed in the air, slowly rotating. Satisfied with the Bridge itself, Cendan knew that the hard part came now. He had to split his concentration, one part keeping the pattern in place for the Bridge, and one to charge block of stone he had brought; to tie the Bridge to it.

"You are ready," Xid whispered, shoring up the tiny ribbon of doubt he had started to feel.

Paying attention to both things at once had been hard to do before in the workroom, and this was just as difficult, if not more so. Blotting out everything else – the sound of the waves, the feeling of the breeze on his skin, even the sound of his breathing – Cendan reached out to the block as-well. Slowly feeding magic into the brick, he formed a new smaller pattern that would tie the block to the raw stuff of magic here. The points of light did not want to go into the block, but they never did. Finding the right amount of force, but not too much, was just as Xid had said; one of the hardest skills in all of this. And one that those who were Creators – call them Makers or Gardeners – were uniquely talented for.

With a snap, the magic stopped fighting him, and with a vibration he swore he heard, flew through the block as if they had always been there.

"Nice job. Now the binding," Xid whispered, careful not to break his concentration. Cendan wasn't listening though; he was wholly bent to the task at hand. Finding the soft point in the Bridge pattern – the one that if he were to pull it out would cause the pattern to collapse – he would join it to the pattern in the stone. Once done, the stone would form a powered base for the marching flow of magic here, and the Bridge would last until the magic of this world went out; which Cendan very much hoped was very far into the future.

Moving the soft point was a dance he decided, a dance of exact measurement. Too hard and the pattern fell; too soft and it would never bind. Sweating as he worked the magic, Xid looked at him with new respect. Cendan had no clue just how powerful he was, but Xid knew. He was the most singularly gifted person born with the creator talent she'd ever met. What he was doing normally took years of practice and failure, and here he was, three or four days in, and making it work! Her mouth compressed into a line. He was still a Bridgefinder though, and the whole reason the world was in danger. The Elder's plan would work, and the other Shrouded, who were foolish enough to want to help his kind, would believe it had been an accident. The Elves were powerful, and what could she do?

The soft point finally fell into place, and just like that, the Bridge was now permanent. A huge grin broke out on Cendan's face. He was nearly done, almost there. Just to join the Bridge here with the Bridge in the Elven village, and he'd be finished. Saying it was easy, but doing it, well… He'd gotten this far. Normally he'd need something from the other side of the Bridge. Xid had told him that was because the magic needed a 'memory' to find the other end. That he didn't have, but he had himself, which apparently was the next best thing. He'd gone through the

Bridge there, and so, he should be able to find it and tie them together. Should being the operative word.

Through his unbound Bridge, Cendan reached out. He was physically still standing on that spit of sand, but his mind flew through the Bridge, trying to home into the Bridge in the Elven village. Thankfully, Xid had been right; it drew him like a beacon. He could see the threads of the Magic here, on the Echo World, tying things together. So odd, similar to the points of light on our world, but still, different enough. He paused, however, when he got a good mental 'look' at the Bridge.

He had forgotten. The Bridge here was banned to Elves. He was totally aware of it now, some film of woven magic overlaying this end of the connection. How did he get past that? He could, as a human, but if the Elves were to be believed, and in this case he was pretty sure they could be, it wouldn't let them through. What could he do? Calm down, he berated himself. Falling back on old skills, he tried to approach this as a job from his old life. This was a system. It used different rules, but it was a system.

The Elves not getting through needed a work around. The workings of the Slyph had caused a... a bug. Think of it like a computer bug, Cendan, a bug he couldn't un-program, but maybe he could bypass. From his end of the Bridge, he sent a small thread of magic through to the Elven side. Xid's breath came sharp.

"What are you doing? That's not part of the pattern!"

Cendan ignored her. He had to keep his concentration; he was juggling multiple patterns across two worlds and trying to explain what was going on was a stretch.

If the magic of the Echo world was laid out in threads, and the threads were woven into magic, which implied a 'cloth' of magic.

Maybe, just maybe, he could force a whole through the woven threads, stretch out a large enough hole for the Elves to use the Bridge. Cendan had no idea if this would work. Truthfully, he was somewhat surprised he could even keep up with everything he was doing right now. Pushing aside all the distractions his mind was coming up with, he took a deep breath and pushed at the film with his thread of earth magic.

Nothing he had ever experienced in his life prepared him for the feeling that hit him the moment the probe like thread hit the Slyph's barrier. Pain? Pleasure? Cold? Hot? He felt like his chest was about to burst from joy, and in the exact same moment his ears were going to explode from a noise that only he could hear. He could feel his concentration slipping, the patterns he was balancing flicker and begin to falter. A low groan escaped Cendan's lips, and he cleared his mind, clearing up the flickering pattern. His probe had made it though. It was through! Now to stretch it out; the hole needed to be bigger. Much bigger.

Quickly working the pattern, he formed the thread into a tube and began to make it wider. The feelings were not nearly as intense though Cendan could very much do without ever feeling that again. Still, his teeth ground together at how massively uncomfortable he felt. Larger still, and the feelings started to fade more.

"Larger," Cendan muttered, forgetting Xid was there at all. All his concentration was used at this point. Larger still the hole went, until finally, he felt certain it would work.

He didn't know if the weaves of that world would return to shape, though, so he had to work fast to combine this tube of his to the Bridge; to keep the way open. It did not escape a corner of his mind that he was working all this, all this work for a race of magical creatures who only wanted to come here to steal horses and human women. He'd shake his head at the irony of it if he could have done.

Xid watched his working with a confused look. What in the hell was Cendan doing? This tube he had formed that wasn't part of the standard Bridge pattern. What was he up to?

She watched as he deftly added this new pattern to the Bridge pattern. His natural skill when he wasn't over-thinking things had asserted itself, and this time the new pattern slid into place without any effort.

Cendan for his part wasn't even paying attention; he was tired, very tired, and starting to fade. Finally, everything was in place for the final binding. He forged a new connection, this time having to draw from the well of magic in his key; the making of the tunnel had exhausted the magic he had gathered at the beginning. 'Just a little more' he told himself, a few more moments.

He could see both ends approaching each other, and then with one final burst of concentration, the connection leapt between the two Bridges. The end points slid together as if they had always been that way. The patterns were stable, they held, and no longer needed Cendan's help. With a feeling of triumph, he released it all and staggered off to the side. He had done it.

"Xid. Let's... get out of here," Cendan said, the note of exhaustion clear in his voice.

Xid stood, eyeing his work.

"Yes. I think that's a good idea; I should get out of here."

Cendan looked up and saw her face. He knew at that moment that she was going to leave him here.

"Xid! What…"

Ignoring him, Xid worked a pattern quickly, faster than he'd ever seen one go, a dance of light flowing out of her fetish. With a nod, Xid vanished, transported back to Rivenwood, leaving him here with an active Bridge to the Echo world; one that led to a group of elves that were going to be very unhappy with his solution to their bargain.

Cendan stood there, stunned. Why had Xid just … well … abandoned him? As he stood there, Rivenwood's warning came back to him: 'not all the Shrouded wanted to help the Bridgefinders'. Gardener Xid must have been one of those, and had simply been waiting, waiting for the right moment to get rid of him. He had to admit he hadn't seen it coming. Xid had never been super-friendly, but she'd not been antagonistic either. His sight registered a slight fluctuation in the Bridge. He didn't have time to sit around and figure out why Xid had left him here.

He had one chance. Just one. The copying pattern. There were two main issues. One: the pattern Xid had used was far more complex that his simple light pattern he'd tried it on before. And secondly, but far more importantly, he didn't even know if it would work. Before he'd been copying a pattern than he had put in place. This would be copying a pattern that someone else had used, and that he hadn't gotten a good look to begin with. With a shudder, the Bridge started to become active, and Cendan knew he had no time to waste.

He was still bone tired; the Bridge's creation had taxed him. The added work needed had even partially drained his focus of its well. He only hoped the well held enough residual magic to make the copying pattern in the first place. Closing his eyes, Cendan worked to ignore the Bridge that was now nearly open. Reaching into his focus, he drew the remaining magic out of the reservoir, and created his new pattern in same general place that Xid had been. He silently said a prayer, praying that this would work.

His eyes snapped open at the sound of a footfall on sand. There, an elf stood, taut and alert, staring at Cendan with golden amber eyes. A hint of a smile crossed the Elf's face until he looked around. Then, turning to Cendan, the once calm face was quickly filled with anger. Whirling towards the Bridge, the Elf yelled something that Cendan couldn't hear or understand; though he must have been the subject because the Elf pointed at Cendan with a hand shaking in anger.

Cendan turned his attention to where he had tried to form the copying pattern. There! Some pattern had formed, and he could only hope it would take him back to the Rivenwood and the Shrouded. Obviously not a safe place either, but not everyone there was out to get him. He ran towards the copied pattern and threw himself towards it with one glance back to the Bridge. King Lachnin and three new Elves were through, and Lachnin was not overly happy to see him. An elf cocked an arrow his way, but Cendan never saw it loose.

Pain engulfed him, worse pain than the travel there. He would later compare the feeling to being on a beach with high winds and being near sandblasted apart. Everything hurt, and all he could do was huddle into a ball as he fell through his tunnel, his tunnel to somewhere. Solid ground greeted him with a heavy thud, and all he could do was groan.

"Cendan!" Heather's voice came to him as the grass he was on tickled his face. He had made it.

Heather ran towards Cendan as he lay on the grass. His clothing smoked, giving off a strange smell, and what she could see of his skin was raw and painful looking. Gardener Xid had taken one look as Cendan came through and ran towards the wood.

"Xid... left me there. Left me to the Elves."

Heather nodded; not that Cendan could see it. She had known there were some vocal members of the Shrouded, backed by some Elders, who wanted nothing to do with trying to help the Bridgefinders. She'd personally been approached by some when the decision to warn the Bridgefinders had been made. She'd been tempted, but had followed Rivenwood's lead.

At first her decision had been one based mostly on saving her own skin. If Grellnot managed to beat the Slyph, something she found to be likely, and then Grellnot defeated the Bridgefinders, then all that raw power would make him very powerful. So powerful that she doubted that the Shrouded could do anything to the thing to stop it. True, there had been some curiosity about the now nearly mythical Bridgefinders. The Shrouded only talked about them in a historical tense, and knowing they were still around, she had wanted to see what all the fuss was about.

She'd not been impressed until she'd entered their headquarters. It was a phenomenal work of magic and skill, one that even she, from a vastly different background, could appreciate. And then there was Cendan. She looked down on the man, on the edge of exhaustion and in pain. Cendan had complicated every damn thing she'd done in the short time she'd known him. Her feelings were confused, her mind was confused, and even her physical responses to the man were confused. She wasn't about to leave him here though. Not at all.

She helped Cendan to his feet though he wasn't totally able to walk right. For once he didn't question her, or what they were doing. As fast as she could, she took him on a different path, toward Rivenwood's tree and away from the direction Xid had gone. Xid was probably already in communion with whatever Elder had put her up to this. Now that they had been exposed, she wasn't sure what else they were going to try, but they would have to do it soon.

"Damn, you are heavier than you look Bridgefinder," Heather muttered. Pausing to lean against a rock, Heather reached through to her fetish to try to find something that would help them move faster. There was no such thing as a flight pattern, to the profound disappointment of generations of young Shrouded casters. Not even a fast travel pattern. But... there! A pattern used to make things easier to move.

Quickly working the pattern, drawing on the stored magic in her fetish, she worked it on the shoes Cendan was wearing. That should at least mean that the dragging would be easier as the pattern would keep his feet from digging into the ground. Heather wished she had time to talk to Rivenwood herself. As it was, she wasn't going to stick around. She was going to take Cendan and get out of here. She didn't know where they would end up, but being away from the rest of the Shrouded, at least while Cendan was under her care, was probably a good thing.

Chapter 19

Grellnot stood on rock, hearing the noises of the creatures he had gathered as they stood behind him. Grellnot cared nothing for them, and they were only there because of their fear. Grellnot could taste it in the air; they were reeking of it. The smell made him hungry, and happy. The foolish things were all going to die when the attack started. Grellnot was no fool, and he could count, for she had far more at her disposal. Even the things behind him – Goblins and Trolls, Jabbers and Xacin, Grublings and Montoes – they loved her just as much as the things that she had gathered.

Grellnot knew some would turn on him, regardless of how many Grellnot ate or threatened to eat. Stupid creatures were just a distraction; something to occupy her defenders so Grellnot could face off against her. The Slyph, one on one. Grellnot felt his hunger grow at the thought of her magic being his, savoring the raw feeling of it, becoming one with Grellnot. The tinkling sound of the Finders shinies on his neck still were comforting, but Grellnot wanted more. Did she even have bones to crunch and savor? Would there be a treasure to hang here on the necklace when he had eaten his fill of her flesh and magic?

Grellnot turned toward his assembled horde.

"Grellnot find you all! You serve Grellnot! Grellnot can smell your fear, your hate." Grellnot spat onto the ground and grinned at the assembled things. The first line shrank back, the rank smell of terror wafting to Grellnot like flowers in a garden. "Grellnot not care. You serve! Or you die."

A large Jabber moaned, its thousand mouths making a noise like a low rumble of thunder.

"Grellnot will lead you onward. The Slyph will die."

Chatter broke out in a group of Grublings, pale worm like things with spider-like legs. Grellnot couldn't understand Grublings, but it didn't matter. Leaping from the rock, Grellnot landed in the midst of the pale things, grabbed the nearest one, and bit it in half. Chewing it slowly, Grellnot heard silence fall over the things he had gathered.

"You fight for Grellnot, or you die." Throwing the body of the Grubling on the ground, he leapt forward, not letting the things behind him see the look of disgust on Grellnot's face. Foul thing; not tasty; no blood. No rich blood, just a pale, pasty, gummy flesh thing.

"Follow!" Grellnot yelled as he heard the things slowly and quietly follow. Grellnot was marching to war.

Exiting the Rivenwood was easier than Heather had hoped it would be. Greenguard let them past without a word, and the pattern she had used made the going a lot simpler. Cendan had regained some strength and was at least helping more as they made their way to his car.

"Why would Xid do that? I mean, I know Rivenwood said some didn't agree, but to leave me there? I just… I don't understand it," Cendan asked out loud, still woozy from everything that had happened. He winced occasionally, his skin still red and painful in places. Heather didn't say anything at first. She kept glancing behind them and making sure they weren't being followed; at least physically. Once they were in the car, she planned on warding the hell out of it, but she didn't want to waste the time now.

"Heather, did you know she was like that?" Cendan asked, finally starting to come fully around. "And what the hell did you do to my feet?" he asked as he almost tripped and fell. "Feels like I'm walking on oiled ice."

Heather sighed. "No of course I didn't know Xid was one of those. You knew there were factions though, some people always have to try to have their way. Xid hid her feelings on the matter well. She must have just been looking for the chance to get rid of you."

Cendan nodded as he stumbled again. "And the feet?"

Heather gave him an eye roll, "You couldn't walk, and you were getting hard to drag around. I used a pattern that reduces friction so that I could actually move you until you could walk on your own."

Cendan gave her an appraising look; that was a rather good idea he knew.

"Well can you undo it? Walking like this is hard. I don't even want to try driving."

Heather closed her eyes for a second, and suddenly the ground felt solid again to Cendan.

"Thanks," Cendan said quickly.

They walked in silence, both glancing back.

"Why aren't they after us?" Cendan muttered. Heather waved her hand in a see saw motion.

"I think, and it's just a guess, that Xid's move to leave you at the mercy of King Lachnin and the Elves was a plan of opportunity. When it failed, they really didn't have a plan to fall back on. And of course, those who want to help you and yours were probably shocked at the attempt. Some may plot behind his back, but no one wants to go up against Rivenwood when he's paying attention." Heather looked behind them as well. "That being said, once we get in the car, I'm going to throw some magical protections up."

The car. Cendan felt like he'd been stuck in a medieval fair for a week and was returning to the real world. The air temperature got warmer as they walked, just as it had gotten cooler closer in. They turned the corner into sunlight, blue skies, hot summer air, and his car.

"Hot," Cendan said out loud, "Got to find a pattern to deal with that!" He flashed a grin as they got in.

An involuntary gasp escaped him as he sat. Parts of his body were still really in pain. Nothing was broken, and he wasn't actually bleeding, but the burning hot car seat against new pink skin was not a feeling he liked. Heather took out her fetish and concentrated. Cendan opened himself to the sight without thinking about it, watching her gather magic from both outside and from the well inside the fetish. Patterns he somewhat recognized as a variation of the warding she had done that first night, on his house, flowed around the car, but with a new twist he'd not seen.

"I see the wards, but what was that last one?" Cendan asked as Heather very quickly put her fetish away.

"Drive, Cendan," Heather motioned him. "That last one will make it harder for anyone to scry out our location while we travel. It can still be penetrated, but that combined with the car in motion will be extra difficult."

Cendan nodded, pulling out of where he had parked several days ago, and heading back towards town.

"Ok so, first things. Where are we going?"

Heather shrugged in response. "Your guess is as good as mine. Your house isn't a great choice; they know where that is."

Cendan nodded. "I'd go back to the Bridgefinders lair, but Marcus is there. Hell, he's probably found a way to block me from coming back. I'm also highly worried about Jasmine. I still think she shouldn't have stayed behind."

Heather opened her mouth to say something, then closed it again. They rode on in silence, Cendan trying to concentrate on driving, rather than the aches and pains he felt or the creeping sense of exhaustion covering him. Heather shifted next to him, nervously fidgeting in her seat.

"So... what if I told you... I... could get us into the Bridgefinders lair? You called it a lair, right?" she blurted out.

Cendan didn't say anything at first, unsure of how to respond. "How?" Was the eventual response.

"Well, when we went in before with... Jasmine, I sort of copied the pattern." She wasn't looking at him, but he could hear the sound of uncertainty in her voice. "Look, I didn't know if I'd need it, and so, as a rule of thumb, I study every pattern I come across, even if I don't think, normally, I'd use it." Head turned toward Cendan, she continued. "I can get us in. Both of us. I'm not letting you out of my sight after what happened the last time. With Marcus I mean."

Cendan slipped into autopilot driving as he tried to think this over. He wasn't surprised she'd copied Jasmine's entry pattern in retrospect, or at least had tried to. He didn't like it though. It was again one of those trust things. Heather had basically taken advantage of him with magic, then taken him to her group, her Shrouded, allowing him to learn more magic in a few days than he'd ever learn on his own. Then she saves him from a faction that wanted him gone, at the same time as now telling him she can break into the Bridgefinders lair. Good and bad, mixed into a great big mess. So typical for him with women. Even with a woman who he wasn't even sure how he felt about.

"Cendan?" Heather asked, cutting into his train of thought again.

"Yeah sorry... I... ok fine. Bridgefinders it is. At least the other Shrouded, or at least the ones who want to get rid of me, can't get in."

Heather snorted. "They won't be after you anymore. Their gambit failed; there's no reason to chase you once you get into the lair again. The whole purpose of that exercise was to block you from taking your training back to the Bridgefinders. Once your back why fight?"

Cendan nodded. She was right though he still felt weird about the whole damn thing.

"Not that your training will help much without Jasmine and Marcus. And they both hate magic," Heather added. "So... I'm going to stick around and help."

Cendan cocked an eyebrow at that. "Oh? Why? I mean, yes we can use the help, but... The Bridgefinders aren't likely to be your cup of tea."

Heather laughed out loud this time. "True, but I've invested too much time in you, Cendan Key, to have you get killed in some stupid way that I could stop."

Unsure of what else to say, Cendan didn't respond, and they rode on in silence. Heather kept taking glances at him, which he ignored for the most part. He could see the growing annoyance on her face each time he didn't say anything though. Cendan didn't know what to say as usual. People, and women, in general were hard to process for him most of the time. Though recent experiences had shown him that if enough other things were going on, his social awkwardness seemed to vanish into the background. But put him here, in a one-on-one situation, and whatever in him that rose to the occasion when things were bad or dangerous, apparently left him totally when riding in a car with a woman he had a highly complicated relationship with.

So in the quiet they rode, Cendan deciding that not saying anything was better than saying the wrong thing, whatever the wrong thing was. Finally, after a long stretch where the only sound was the tires on the road, they parked near to the Red Orchid. Cendan half wondered if the entrance had been moved since he'd been gone. Jasmine would have most likely told him if that was the case, he hoped.

"Before we go in, I want to fill the well back up in my focus. I honestly don't know what we are going to find in there. Add to the fact that I hurt all over, I'm tired, and I'm sick of people trying to kill me, I want to be ready for whatever," Cendan added, looking around.

Heather nodded, but didn't say anything back; her face blank. Cendan sighed to himself. Maybe not saying anything had been the wrong thing. Reaching out, Cendan slowly made the pattern to refill the focus, feeling the decidedly different 'taste' of the magic here. Out in the Rivenwood, things had a rough feel, he realized, somewhat random and unsettled. Here in the city, and by the Bridgefinders lair, the magic had a different feel. He couldn't put his finger on it; it just felt, more organized and more predictable.

"You ready?" Heather asked, after some time had passed. Cendan had been silent, eyes closed. Slowly nodding, Cendan readied himself. He'd actually already filled his focus, and had been searching through the saved patterns on the Key, looking for anything that might help him feel better. There was one that might help, but since he didn't want to get into finding all the old patterns from Oakheart yet, he wanted to wait until he was alone to actually try it. And maybe after a good meal, and a really long nap. His stomach growled at him a bit in protest.

He'd had lunch, but that had been prior to the work on the Bridge and the whole crazy situation with Xid. At least the lair had a fully stocked kitchen. As they walked, the half block to the back stairs that led down to the transition point, Cendan wondered how far Jasmine had gotten with Marcus. The fact that he hadn't heard anything didn't mean much. He had been in Rivenwood, not exactly a mecca of cellular phone connections. However, turning the corner, he saw the car Jasmine had been driving that night when she'd come back with Heather, still parked in exactly the same spot. It hadn't moved. That wasn't a good sign.

"Should that be there still?" Heather asked, pointing to the vehicle.

"No. It shouldn't be. The fact that is… I don't know what it means, but it's not a good thing," Cendan answered.

"Gotcha. Sounds like fun," she responded in a deadpan way. He wasn't sure if she was trying to be funny or not, but the slight attempt at humor did reduce the feeling of stress he was starting to feel.

"Well, at least we won't get attacked with Magic. Marcus doesn't use the stuff. Is there a pattern to deal with more physical stuff? I would prefer not to get cold cocked again, and even less so today. If you didn't know, I don't think it's been a terribly great one." Cendan waved his hand towards his body. "Not really up to snuff."

Heather laughed again. The slight tension that had existed since her comment in the car mostly evaporated now in their shared need to find some way to deal with the unknown situation they were about to get into. The outer door leading down to the transition point was open as well and looked like it hadn't been closed either in the days that Cendan had been gone. A small, drying water puddle from a rain storm had formed, and some loose trash had blown in. Not a good sign either. Was the way into the lair still even here?

As they stood in front of the wall, they exchanged glances. Cendan held his focus in his hand and reached out. Yes! The transition point was still there. He, however, couldn't open it. Every time he tried, it just slid away from him.

"Ok, so it's still here, but I'm barred from opening it. I wondered if Marcus might find a way to keep me from coming back. Go ahead and try what you can," Cendan asked Heather, opening his eyes to the sight. He wanted to see this, see if he could try to follow the pattern.

His sight blossomed in front of him as he watched a folded and waved pattern form around them. The transition point itself he'd never looked at with the sight, and he noted its distinct similarities to a Bridge; but still some clear differences. What would change when he tried to open it? But with the sense of unease here with the car and the open door, he knew it was better to get in and see what was going on. He watched as the pattern Heather had created seemed to connect to the transition in a strange way, and then just as quick the way was open.

"C'mon. I don't know if Marcus or Jasmine can tell I did that, but I'd rather find out inside than outside," Heather remarked as they each took a breath and walked forward.

The inside looked pretty much the same; or at least the entrance did. Still the same randomness as always. Nothing seemed out of place, but it would be hard to make anything look different here. At least he knew now why the Maker wing information about the place had stressed that patterns had power. One mystery solved at least; a minor victory, but better than before.

"Ok, we are in. Before we go further, I can ward us against one physical blow. Just one. People are hard to ward; we move too much," Heather noted.

Once again she quickly worked a pattern, this one settling over them both before slowly sinking into their skin. Cendan noted with a level of professional interest that she appeared to tie the pattern to her fetish, and at the same time she worked a recharge pattern into it, effectively keeping the pattern running off her fetish, but not draining it.

"Neat trick," Cendan said.

"Yeah, the ward is a good one to know. I'll show you in more detail after we figure out everything," she replied and gripped her fetish in one hand. "Lead the way. You know this place better than I."

Cendan headed down the hall, keeping his eyes and ears open. He did let go of the sight, however; it was a bit distracting here in a fairly magic rich environment.

"Wait, EVA!" He reached out towards the presence in his mind that had been so quiet as of late. It was still there, but barely. Sadly, he couldn't even feel that she was there without concentration. He felt a bit guilty honestly; he hadn't even been thinking about her while he was in the Rivenwood. There'd been so much to learn and know, he'd kind of forgotten her. Which bothered him. Why and how could he forget EVA?

"Anything?" Heather asked beside him. "If that mechanical thing can help us, or tell us what's been going on here, that would be useful."

Cendan's shoulders shrugged. "I can't feel her, well only barely." He debated calling out for Jasmine, but again, he wanted to find her before dealing with Marcus. "Let's go to the kitchen. At least there's a better chance she is there than Marcus is. Unless something drastic has changed in the last few days, he's probably holed up in the barrier room." Cendan walked down the hall, but taking care not to make much noise.

They passed by the map room on the way, still left in exactly the same way as it had been. The ragged hole was still in the wood.

"I never found a way to fix that," Cendan said, stopping to look.

"All in good time. I don't think any of us expected things to go south like this, Cendan." Heather's hand fell on his shoulder, a small comfort. Cendan thought back to that day, not too long ago in time, but an eternity in experience and knowledge. He shrugged off her hand, remembering what had happened later. Not speaking, he returned the way he had been going, Heather following behind.

Cendan's fears amplified as they turned the corner and saw what the kitchen had become. It was a wreck. Smashed cabinets; food thrown on the floor; something or someone had trashed the place. Burn marks on the wall from something, and food just thrown away and rotting, based on the smell coming from the trash. His hunger faded as he took it in, replaced by a growing worry about Jasmine.

"Someone did a number on this place," Heather said out loud. "And that doesn't seem like a good sign for you or me."

"Yeah, or Jasmine, assuming that Marcus had something to do with this," Cendan responded, tightening his grip on the key. "Let's keep moving."

He started off down a side hall, heading straight to EVA's main room. Hopefully the connection would work better there. Hopefully. And barring finding Jasmine on the way, he might get some answers. The door to EVA's room seemed normal, but the room itself was not. Spare parts from the Maker wing were all over the place, some burst and broken, and a ladder was placed directly where Cendan knew there was a secret keyhole.

"This shouldn't look like this," Cendan said to Heather, who was standing behind him with a somewhat awed expression.

Reaching out again for EVA, he noted the connection was stronger here, which he had strongly hoped.

"EVA, can you hear me?" Cendan asked mentally. No words came out, but a throb of gratitude and excitement seemed to pulse off the thing in his mind. "Can you tell me, or show me, where Jasmine is? I need to know what's been going on. I can tell someone has been doing... something to you, and I'm going to assume its Marcus?" The tiny piece of EVA flashed in strong anger at the mention of Marcus's name. Or was that pain? Hurt? He wasn't sure how much EVA could actually feel. "I'll do whatever I can to help you, but we've got to find Jasmine."

The air around them both seemed to tense up and thicken, and in the tiniest of whispers, he heard a tiny reedy voice say, 'Exam Room...' Heather nodded at him.

"I heard it to. You know where that is?" He nodded, holding up a finger for her to wait a moment.

"EVA, I'll be back. Can you tell me anything about what's happened?" Anger and fear flooded through their link. Cendan knew that if it was this strong with whatever had happened to dampen it, EVA was in fact terrified. "Calm EVA, calm. I get it. I'll be back, and I'll be careful!" he said out loud for Heather's benefit.

He pointed down the hall, leading the way as they walked. As they traveled, he explained what EVA had been feeling.

"Great, so the magical mechanical everything is terrified. This doesn't make me feel any better, Cendan!" Heather said as she shifted her now white knuckled grip on her fetish.

Cendan agreed with her. EVA being worried wasn't a good thing.

"The exam rooms aren't far. But the fact that EVA thinks Jasmine is there is not good news. Those rooms haven't been used in ages. They were... primitive rooms used for the study and who knows what else on creatures from the Echo World."

Marcus was still the unknown quantity, but based on what they already had seen and knew, Jasmine hadn't been able to do anything about him. Cendan was worried now that in fact the rage and anger that had been directed at him had, in his absence, been directed at Jasmine.

"Just around this corner," Cendan said as they walked faster. Turning the corner, the door to the primary exam room was open a crack. Heather cocked her head for a second and motioned Cendan to be quiet. Silence filled the hall, but was that breathing he heard?

Chapter 20

Slowly they walked toward the cracked open door and peeked in. Jasmine! They both burst into the room, and as Cendan saw Jasmine, his stomach sank. She was still wearing the same clothing that he'd last seen her in. She was sweaty, dirty and very pale. Marcus had shackled her to the table as well, it appeared. Anger rose in him, both at Marcus and at himself. He should have convinced her to leave with him, not this! Heather had turned somewhat pale taking this all in, as well.

"Cendan. We need to get her out of here, but you need to know… There's a pattern here. She's under a spell."

Cendan brought forth his sight, swearing under his breath. Heather was right. There was a pattern, flowing into her head and out of it, and oddly the pattern was somehow attached to, well, everything. Unlike what the Shrouded had taught him, this pattern was locked in multiple ways in both points and threads.

"This is weird," Heather mumbled. "I've seen a lot, and I've never seen anything like this one."

Cendan nodded. "I don't know if we can do anything about it, but let's get her out of here at least." As he quickly undid the shackles, out of the corner of his eye, he saw her focus; the painted red orchid. Why wasn't this in the barrier room? Marcus had always insisted on them being there.

"Cendan there's something else you're not realizing. This pattern; the only other person who could have done this is Marcus. That means he's using magic. Which means… we are in far more danger than we thought."

His movements slowed as the awareness of what Heather was saying sunk in. Marcus hated magic. He hated the very thought of magic. But yet, here was proof he was using patterns. He was using the very magic he had complained – screamed even – about.

"We are in deep here..." Cendan noted.

"EVA!" he said out loud while he worked the last of the restraints off of Jasmine's unconscious form. "I bet that whatever is going on with EVA, that's Marcus's doing as well."

Heather nodded as she kept her eye on the door.

"That makes sense. But how could he do these things? I mean, he's had no training. And even the Shrouded know that Marcus hates the stuff; magic I mean."

Cendan slowly picked Jasmine up, her body limp and deadweight.

"I don't know how. But I'm not sure finding out how is going to be an experience I will enjoy. Keep an eye out for Marcus. Let's get Jasmine out of here. And us to for that matter!" Cendan waved to Jasmine's focus, "Can you get that? Don't want to leave it here."

Heather took it, her practiced eye knowing what it was.

The hallway looked the same though Cendan felt like everything had a more sinister feeling to it now. Where was Marcus? None of this made any sense, and Jasmine, the only person who might shed some light on what the hell was going on, was stone cold out of it. Heather followed behind him if only because she didn't know the way. The going was slow. Cendan's grip kept slipping. Carrying someone who was truly deadweight was far harder than it looked, and Jasmine didn't even weigh that much. Cendan tried to make light of it, to diffuse his tension at least.

"Ok, once we are safe, I gotta come up with a pattern for making things easier to carry!" His attempt at humor fell flat, though, even to himself.

Three corners, two, one, and there they were at the exit.

"Go on, let's get out of here!" Cendan said as Heather raised her fetish. A pause, and then she slowly lowered it, her face turning even paler.

"Cendan, I can't. He knows we are here. It's barred!"

Cendan swore again to himself. Locked up in a place they can't leave with a violent crazy man, who has unknown magical abilities.

"Damn it," Cendan swore, still holding Jasmine. "What the hell now?"

Marcus's face split into a grin. The traitor Cendan and that witch were now trapped. He had been surprised when they had entered, shocked in fact. The Keystone had alerted him to Jasmine entering the lair. He'd sprinted to see how she'd escaped, only to find her still bound in place and unconscious. It was only then, using the abilities of the Keystone, he had realized that somehow Cendan and the witch woman from before had found a way to mimic Jasmine's entry.

Anger had spread through him, and at first he'd wanted to use his new abilities to hurt them, make them feel all the pain they had inflicted upon him. Only one thing had stopped him; Cendan's focus. That key was the way to end the war with the

Slyph, forever. That would make him the hero and the legend. He didn't want to damage it; Cendan always had his focus with him. Always. Just another betrayal of how the Bridgefinders worked. Cendan was 'too good' to leave his key to help strengthen the barrier.

He had to find a way to get it away from him. He needed it, and he desired it. Cendan wasn't worthy of even touching it. He'd watched as they found Jasmine, hidden away but watching. Somehow the Keystone allowed him to see everything and anything in the headquarters, and he used it to great effect.

The first thing was to lock the door; they couldn't get out, and they had to stay. Watching Cendan struggle with carrying Jasmine, his first delight turned to disgust. He didn't use magic! Watching and listening to the witch and the traitor talk about using the tool of the Slyph, turned his stomach. He was using the powers granted to him by being the Leader of the Bridgefinders. Nothing more and nothing less.

The witch was cute enough, he thought as he watched them, even for all her lies and deceit. The story about Grellnot and the Slyph at war were all lies, he was sure. Lies and tricks, designed to have them let one of the outsiders in, to let them destroy what was left of the Bridgefinders. That witch probably took the orders from the Slyph herself, to lie low the mighty Bridgefinders once and for all. The weak ones had fallen for it. Cendan was even helping them! But not Marcus; no, Marcus knew the truth. There was no war on the Echo World, and the Slyph was making her final move. She'd tried a straight attack which had failed. This plan of hers was subterfuge and poison.

Marcus turned his attention back to the traitor as they realized Marcus had trapped them, trapped them in a maze that they didn't know he controlled.

"You will die soon, Cendan Key, you and that witch. I'll take your focus and use it. And my name, Marcus Wheeldon, will go down in history as the man who defeated the Slyph. I will win." Marcus spat the words out and huddled around the Keystone. His Keystone.

He just had to wait. He needed to find a way to get that key away from Cendan. They wouldn't find him, and he'd know where they were at all times. That witch though, he didn't need her, he didn't need her at all. The grin returned to his face. Marcus was going to have some fun.

The two armies faced each other, one dwarfed by the other. Grellnot's conscripted force, for all its size, was nothing compared to the sheer numbers the Slyph had. Even now, Grellnot could hear the things behind him grumbling. Fear kept them in line, and not just fear for their own lives, but what Grellnot could do to their tribes, homes, even their whole race. The Slyph did not stand at the head of her forces, but at the back. Grellnot could smell her. She was confident, proud. The two creatures near her were new to Grellnot, and their smell confused him. He peered to see the magic, the threads themselves.

All of the assembled things were overlaid with it, it was bound to their very beings. And all ties for them led back to her. Grellnot suffered a rare shock, however when looking at the two hounds; they were like Grellnot! A mix of the magic of this world and the magic of the human world. Grellnot did not know where they came from, but they did not give Grellnot much worry. They were flesh and bone. They could be eaten, just like everything else.

"Grellnot!" The Slyph's voice burst out over the plain, as the creatures silenced themselves. Even the ones Grellnot had gathered still worshiped the Slyph as a goddess. "Grellnot! How dare you turn against me? I, who created you; I who gave you the power to hunt the humans. And yet here you are, daring to strike at me?"

Grellnot smiled, his long tongue hanging low like a panting dog.

"GRELLNOT HUNGERS!" he screamed back. "Grellnot not be your slave, Grellnot not need your help or power. Gellnot is power."

Lurching forward faster than any creature, save the Slyph, could follow, Grellnot tore the head off a giant bull looking creature – that is if a bull was covered with metal skin and breathed smoke. Tearing chunks of steaming hot flesh off the body of the thing, Grellnot took huge bites.

"GRELLNOT HUNGERS!" It screamed again.

"I will destroy you Grellnot!" The Slyph had no need to scream, her voice carried over the air as if she was standing next to each creature there. "You have outlived your usefulness, creature." Standing in the air, the Slyph raised her hand to order the attack.

"You have no power over Grellnot," Grellnot screamed back. "Show them. Destroy me from there."

Creatures on both sides watched the Slyph, expecting her to destroy Grellnot with a flick of her hand. But she did not. Muttering arose.

"SHOW THEM," Grellnot screamed again. "She cannot hurt Gellnot." Dancing on the corpse of the thing he had just killed, Grellnot howled with glee. "She can't hurt Grellnot. She wants her pets to do it, she is too scared of Grellnot!"

Again the creatures looked to the Slyph to destroy Grellnot. The sky darkened over them as the Slyph grew angry.

"KILL HIM!" she yelled, ordering her creatures to attack.

Grellnot simply pointed at the Slyph, and with a roar, Grellnot moved forward, his army reluctantly following. Most had expected not to have to fight; that the Slyph would end him. They had hoped she'd forgive them for following Grellnot. The two armies clashed and thought ended. Now was the time to fight, or die.

Time passed, and chaos ruled. Jabber fought Jabber, goblins speared anything that came close, and no one and nothing knew friend from foe.

Grellnot paid the things following it no mind. Grellnot had one goal; to get to the Slyph and to feast. Stomach growling in its ever present hunger, Grellnot leaped from creature to creature, ripping out throats, biting through muscle and sinew. Not knowing or caring on which side any creature was. They were all meat, food, blood. Grellnot's hunger grew with each kill.

The Slyph watched Grellnot move through the battlefield. This had been a mistake, Grellnot was a danger she didn't have an answer to. She had hoped the sheer number of creatures could overwhelm the thing, but was quickly shown that that idea was one she never should have had.

"Hounds! Defend me!" The Slyph sent her two pets after Grellnot and vanished from the field of battle.

Grellnot saw the Slyph flee, and could feel her location elsewhere.

'She flees," he screamed, his voice so loud it overwhelmed the noise of battle, sending many things to the ground clutching ears or whatever else they used to hear with. "She flees!" Grellnot screamed again. Confusion spread over the great battle. A great many simply left, to return to wherever they had come from, fearful and unsure of what to do. Some still fought, too lost in bloodlust to be aware of anything else.

A baying noise broke into Grellnots celebration. T hose creatures, the new ones, ran towards Grellnot. He could smell the magic that made them, so similar to Grellnot. Grellnot was greater though, Grellnot had more. More power, more strength, more hunger! With a scream of joy, Grellnot ran at the hounds, blood and flesh, magic and power; Grellnot would feast!

The Slyph appeared far off, in a safe hold she had recently made. She'd spent the last day or so traveling over the Echo world, making places to hide if it came to that. Hide. Her, the Slyph, hiding from a disgusting thing like Grellnot. Regret was not something the Slyph felt often, but with every fiber of her being she regretted making that thing. She paced around the smooth underground hollow she had made, waiting. A forceful lurch shook the hollow, and she whirled around.

Grellnot stood, his face locked into a rictus smile, blood dripping from most parts of its body.

"Grellnot find you…." it said in an almost sing song way. "Grellnot feast on your poor dogs. They were tasty, and so like Grellnot." It flicked a small piece of something towards the

Slyph, and she dodged out of the way. It was a part of a tentacle, from one of her hounds.

The Slyph felt fear, something she had no experience with.

"Grellnot, we are not enemies. The humans are, the Bridgefinders. They are the enemy."

Grellnot laughed, a deep rough sound, and licked its lips, savoring the taste of her fear. The Slyph's fear. Grellnot wanted more.

"Humans are food. Meat and bone, blood and sinew. Grellnot not fear them, Grellnot eat them."

The Slyph slowly walked backward, away from the thing she had created.

"Yes, food Grellnot. So why are you here? Go… hunt! I release you from your banishment. You can go back to the human world and eat your fill!" Just as quickly as she had sealed the Barrier from letting him through, she ended it.

Grellnot shook its greasy head. "Grellnot will hunt, Grellnot will feast. But the Slyph will be first. Grellnot is free now, Grellnot is not your tool!" Screaming in rage, Grellnot leaped again for the Slyph, but with a blink and a rush of inward moving air, the Slyph was gone, transported elsewhere. Grellnot spat on the floor.

"She can't run from Grellnot, Grellnot will find yoooouu…." Its voice, moments ago filled with rage, was once again a sweet croon. Grellnot raised its head and smiled, then it vanished, leaving nothing but an empty hole in the ground behind.

The Slyph appeared in a different place, and in her rush, almost didn't recognize it. The ground was burned and cracked, and the burned out ruined husk of a huge oak tree stood over it all. Oakhearts tree. She hadn't returned here since her anger at his mind and spirit letting go. The Slyph touched a blackened section of bark, wishing Oakheart was still here. The Slyph did not regret what she had done to him, but she wished she had his power. Being able to draw on the magic of the human world might be of use to her when it came to her new enemy.

If Cendan Key hadn't managed to escape, she would have had a new Maker to play with, maybe even two if she had caught him early enough. She still wasn't sure how he had managed to escape. Bridges between the worlds weren't that common. She suspected that he had been helped by something or someone here, and that list was not very long; those who would help a human.

A soft pop behind her let her know her time of reflection was up. Grellnot had arrived.

"Grellnot will always find you. You cannot run from Grellnot!" its rasping voice came. "The tree? You not happy when the other stupid human Maker stole the tree away from you, it looks like. Smells like death to Grellnot."

Turning toward the creature, the Slyph felt fear once more, but tamed it as best she could. She was the Slyph! She was the ruler of this world, creator of life here, master of all she saw.

Grellnot was sitting on a burned rock, picking its teeth with a small piece of bone it had produced from somewhere.

"You cannot run from Grellnot. Grellnot finds the idea of eating you here, where Grellnot was born, a good one." Drool spilled down from the corner of its mouth, stringy and thick. "Your time is gone. Grellnot will rule."

Holding up both hands, the Slyph knew this was it. She had to either stop Grellnot here, or she would die. She could not die to this thing. This stomach with teeth.

"Listen to me, I am your creator! I am your mother! You only exist because of me!"

Grellnot stood saying nothing at first.

"Tell me, do you bleed? Grellnot wants to know."

The Slyph could see the rising hunger and rage reflected in its eyes.

"Grellnot…" the Slyph started to say, then she lashed out as hard as she could with all the power she had been gathering since the thing appeared. Weaves of threads tore through the space between them, trying to find some purchase, some way to unmake this thing.

Grellnot shook itself. She was trying to hurt Grellnot!

Its skin burned, and the air around Grellnot grew thick. Each step was agony, and it would have roared in pain if it could open its mouth. Grellnot was more than of this world though. Grellnot was of both worlds, and that saved it. The threads could not make purchase, the points and specks of light that made up the human world magic simply made the threads slide off of Grellnot. She could hurt Grellnot, she could slow Grellnot, but the Slyph could not kill Grellnot!

The Slyph felt her fear return, a feeling she hated herself for having. Her magic wasn't working! Unlike the magic of humans, her magic, the magic of this world, followed different rules. The threads weren't unraveling, they weren't ending. It was bound too tight, too dense for even her, born of this world before all others, to break the wave.

Compressing its rage and hate, Grellnot ran through the weaves the Slyph was throwing at it, bursting through with a thunderclap. Its jaws crunched down on the neck of the Slyph and began to feed. The air grew still as the blood filled its mouth. Blood rich with magic and power. Grellnot could scream with the joy it gave Grellnot to eat of it. Silence fell, moving outward across the plains and mountains, forests and swamps, caves and seas.

Creatures and nameless things alike could feel it. All raised their heads and were afraid. Grellnot had won.

Chapter 21

Grellnot could not feel anything but the power now, connecting it to every living thing on the Echo World. And all was Grellnot's to command. The air, the sun in the sky, the earth beneath its feet. Darkness fell, a darkness split by howling winds and powerful storms.

"Grellnot has FEASTED!" It screamed into the falling dark, its joy a palpable thing.

The corpse of the Slyph was thin now, a desiccated fragile thing. She had only been filled with the power; no flesh to tear, no bone to crack.

"Unsatisfying," Grellnot muttered as he flung what was left of the Slyph at the base of the oak tree. "She was right about one thing; humans are good to eat." Grellnot laughed out loud. Reaching out with its new power, Grellnot summoned a new army, an army twice, three times as large.

"Grellnot commands you now! Come to Grellnot. Tonight we win!" Grellnot yelled, the joy in its voice overlaying the storm sounds. And the creatures came, big and small, many Grellnot knew, but many it did not. Nameless things from deep underground, blind, but possessed of deep cunning. Flying monsters that were legend even here, on the Echo World. Grellnot's world.

Grellnot smiled. The time was coming. The Slyph had lost because the Slyph did not understand hunger or destruction. Grellnot would feast on the human world, feast on its magic, feast on its humans and animals. Even now its hunger returned, a groaning need to rend and tear. With a slash of a clawed and gnarled hand, Bridges opened up above the still appearing creatures.

"HUNT! KILL! FEAST!" Grellnot screamed as it leaped forward into the closest Bridge. The time had come.

Cendan sat on the bed in his old room at the Bridgefinders liar. They were locked in, apparently, by a completely insane Marcus. Jasmine was still out, and he and Heather had no idea where Marcus was, or what his next move would be.

"We need to wake her. She may at least be able to tell us something," Heather said, looking at Jasmine. "And I think we are going to want her help if Marcus does move against us." She was right, but it made him feel like a character from a TV show where they wake some poor slob up to answer questions when all the person wants is to sleep.

"I know. But Jasmine can't help, with the magic, I mean... she doesn't know any of it. Hell, she doesn't believe in it, though not with the same level of hate and fear that Marcus does, or did." Cendan looked down at her. "But either way, you're right. If nothing else, maybe we can get some food and water into her. She really doesn't look good to me." Standing, he held his key over Jasmine's sleeping form. "I don't know what to do, though."

Heather gently placed her hand on his and pushed it down.

"Let me handle this. You're powerful, Cendan, but this doesn't require brute force. Guard the door."

Cendan reluctantly nodded. Jasmine was his friend of course, but Heather knew far more about magic than he did. He had already searched through the saved patterns on the Key from Oakheart, and nothing seemed like it would help in this case.

"You think you can wake her up?"

Heather shrugged. "Truthfully? Not sure. I don't really know what he did here. That being said, I have a lot more practice than you at magic. So the only way to know is to try."

Cendan didn't like it, but he knew that Heather was right.

"Just be careful, ok? Jasmine is… Jasmine is about the only ally we have here." He wanted to say more, but the whole situation between him, Jasmine and Heather was nebulous at best. There may not even be anything there for all he knew, and even if there was, this wasn't the time or place to get into it.

To her credit, Heather didn't make any half snide comments. She simply closed her eyes, and lightly took her fetish in each hand, touching it with her fingertips only. Cendan watched with both professional and personal interest. He noted that Heather often held her fetish differently based on what she was doing; was that doing something? Or was it just personal preference? Heather drew the surrounding magic, spinning a pattern that seemed to intersect with each thread of light that connected Jasmine to the lair itself.

"Ok, if this works, I'll break every connection at once. That, hopefully, will free her from this trance she's in. There's also a very good possibility that Marcus will know about this the moment I do it," Heather said, her tone firm. "Oh, and Cendan, this is going to hurt. A lot."

Cendan started to object when Heather ripped the pattern back, breaking each thread. The pattern around Jasmine fell apart instantly, and just as fast, Heather tensed up, her breath came in a sharp intake, and she collapsed hard on the floor.

"Heather!" Cendan moved towards her quickly, unsure of what he could do.

"Ow," Heather mumbled. "That hurt like a son of a bitch." Cendan helped her up as Heather winced and rubbed her temples. "Did the pattern break? My head hurts too much to use the sight," Heather asked, as she sat on the edge of the bed.

"Yeah, it looks like it," Cendan answered. "I know you said it wasn't easy to break someone else's pattern, but aside from the pain, it didn't look too hard."

Heather shook her head. "Normally it is harder. That pattern was, well, just odd. I can't think of any other way to say it. And the pain is bad, my head still aches."

Cendan checked on Jasmine again and Heather nursed the headache she had. He noticed immediately that her color was back, and she was breathing more deeply.

"She looks better. Do you think I should try to wake her up now?"

Heather just shrugged in response. She didn't really know Jasmine, so she couldn't say how she'd react, even if she did wake up now. Cendan, not getting an answer, let out a slow breath.

"Here goes nothing," he whispered, and gently shook Jasmine. "Jasmine, can you hear me?"

Her reaction was swift and terrifying. Her body tensed up, then compressed into a ball, and a low moan escaped her.

"No no no no no," was all Jasmine was saying, over and over again.

"Jasmine, it's me, Cendan!" Cendan was shocked. What had Marcus done to her? "Jasmine, you're safe…"

Jasmine's eyes flickered to Cendan, then Heather.

"Cendan? What… How are you here? Where am I…? Marcus! Oh god, Marcus!" Her eyes snapped shut. "How did we get out of the headquarters?"

Cendan looked at Heather then sighed.

"We didn't. We are still here. We are… locked in."

Jasmine's eyes shot open. "That means he can… Cendan we have to get out. You don't understand. Marcus is, he can…" Tears appeared in her eyes. Cendan's shock turned to deep worry. What in the hell was going on?

"Jasmine, we will do all we can to get out, but I need to know what happened. Heather and I both do." Jasmine nodded slowly, trying to calm down.

"Ok… look…" She sniffed a bit, her tears stopping. "Look, Marcus is insane. Totally insane. He's got something he calls the Keystone. It's somehow part of this place, something only he can use as the leader of the Bridgefinders. He's gone crazy. He hates you, Cendan, and with that Keystone he can… He can do things to your mind; things to your soul."

Cendan just reached down and hugged her. "You don't need to say what he did, Jasmine, it's ok."

"No! It's not ok!" Jasmine yelled. "Marcus… He didn't physically touch me, but… in my mind… Oh god…" Tears came again, and Cendan was silent this time. What could he say? Heather had opened her eyes by this time, and the look on her face was one of stony resolve.

"Cendan, if he's got something that can control this place, then he knows where we are, and that lock on the door isn't going to stop him." Cendan felt his stomach drop. How bad could things get?

Jasmine's voice, broken and hurt, cut in.

"It is worse. He's watching us, right now. That Keystone lets him. I don't know why, Cendan, but he wanted you back here. He wants something from you."

Cendan swallowed in fear. "Do you have any idea what? Or why?"

Jasmine shook her head. "I just know he hates you. Hates you," Jasmine whispered quietly, her body still huddled into a ball.

"Cendan, if he's watching us right now, how are we going to get out of here?" Heather asked.

Cendan shook his head in response. He didn't have a damn clue. What was this Keystone thing anyways? When he'd last seen Marcus, he'd been unhinged, but this was way past that. Sitting in silence still holding Jasmine, Cendan considered what few options they had. Sitting in his room here wasn't going to get them anything if Marcus could see and hear everything they were doing. They could try to break out forcefully, but he doubted that would work. Even if Jasmine could be shown enough to help them, he wasn't sure she was mentally up to the task at the moment.

There was one option, but he hated it.

"MARCUS!" he yelled out loud, startling both Heather and Jasmine. "I know you can hear me. Let Heather and Jasmine go, and I'll stay. You wanted me anyways, right? I'll stay."

Heather started to say something and stopped herself, but her face, which moments before had been stone and calm, now showed her concern. Jasmine's reaction was stronger.

"Cendan, you can't stay! You don't know what he can do. What he will do."

Cendan nodded. "I know. But that gets you out of here, and Heather. Maybe with some help from the Shrouded, you all can get me out too, but I can't think of anything else to do."

Jasmine looked confused at the name of the Shrouded, but didn't answer.

"I don't like it, Cendan. You're right, but I don't like it," Heather said. "How can we know he's going to agree anyways?"

Cendan sighed in response, his shoulders slumped.

"I guess we go to the entrance and see. Staying here doesn't get us anything. I hate it. I hate being powerless like this."

Heather stood. "I hate it too, but you are not powerless, Cendan Key." She slowly nodded to him. Cendan knew she was right, and why she wasn't saying anything. The less the watching Marcus knew about what he'd learned already, the better.

Jasmine, however, didn't know and showed it.

"There has to be a better way, Cendan. This is crazy! You don't know what he's become."

Cendan felt his face fall. "I know. But look; before, you stayed to try to talk some sense into him. Now, I'm the one to stay to try to talk some sense into him. We trade positions that's all." Cracking a smile, Cendan tried to put a brave face on all of this. "I don't know what else we can do. He wants me, so I'll give him me. Too much other stuff going on, Jasmine. Heather will tell you once you're out."

A glance exchanged between Jasmine and Heather made it clear they didn't particularly trust each other. That was fine, they needed to get out.

"Marcus! We are heading to the exit. Let them out and I'll stay," Cendan yelled out again as they left his room and headed down the hall, Heather and Jasmine in the lead, and Cendan behind.

"Heather, if this works, take Jasmine back to my place. She can get cleaned up and eat something; fill her in on everything as well. I'll do everything in my power to get out of here as well. Everything I can, at least."

The entrance to the lair stood before them, the same solid wall. Once that seemed so normal. Now took on a somewhat sinister cast.

Jasmine broke her silence.

"My focus!" She patted herself down, and Heather reached into a pocket somewhere and pulled out the carved wooden flower.

"No worries. Here it is."

Jasmine grabbed it and relaxed somewhat as soon as she had it.

"Ok Heather." Cendan motioned at the door looking around.

"Cendan, she can't..." Jasmine started to say before she cut off watching the exit with an expression of worry and surprise. "How did she do that?"

Marcus had kept his side of the bargain, apparently, to Cendan's apparent relief.

"It's still barred to you, Cendan. Are you sure you want to do this?" Heather asked. "I and Rivenwood have a lot riding on you. This is a distraction from the true threat."

Nodding, Cendan reached into his pocket and held his focus.

"I know. But I can't think of anything else at the moment. It's better to get you all out and maybe think of something. You know what I can do." Cendan flashed a smile at Heather. In all actuality, Heather only knew a tiny bit of what he could do. Oakheart's stored patterns would, he hoped, give him an edge on all this. "Besides, if I can stop Marcus, maybe I can undo anything he did to EVA. And in the larger fight, EVA will be useful; very useful."

Jasmine knew there was more not being said than was being said, but kept her mouth shut.

"Let's go, Jasmine," Heather said and walked through the transition point. Jasmine turned to Cendan.

"Be careful. Marcus Wheeldon is not the same person he once was. Whatever that Keystone thing is, it's warped him. He's...." Trailing off, Jasmine gave Cendan a hug. "Stay safe."

And she turned, following Heather to the outside, to freedom.

"Yeah, stay safe," Cendan mumbled to himself. He turned towards the long hall in front of him. Opening himself up to the sight, Cendan quickly ran through the stored patterns. He worked the patterns he thought that might help quickly. Even ones he wasn't totally sure what they did. He copied the one Heather had worked before, the one that protected against a physical attack, adding to it ones he thought, maybe, might disrupt a spell or two that Marcus might throw his way.

He needed to get to the Maker wing. If he was going to find anything out about this Keystone thing that would be the place to start. Holding his focus tight, he headed that way, avoiding the larger rooms where maybe Marcus could attack him easier. The only sound he heard was his own footsteps. All else was still, silent. Even the barrier room door, as he passed it by, showed nothing. All the lights were out.

For a split second he debated entering that room and seeing if Marcus was there. It had always been one of his favorite places. Finding out about the Keystone was more important though. Cendan needed information. Information on what he was dealing with, and why Marcus had gone off the deep end.

The Maker wing was in a state when Cendan arrived. Books thrown all over the place, torn pages, and store rooms where things had been knocked off shelves.

"Great. A mess!" Cendan grumbled. He started searching through the books, looking for anything that mentioned the Keystone. He figured that Marcus must have found out about it here. There wasn't any mention of it before Cendan had opened this area up.

Finally, thirty minutes into his search, he found it. As he read, he knew what had happened, and why. The Keystone had been created to be a focus. A focus 'plus', Cendan liked to think of it as. The plus part being its ability to control the headquarters, completely. And anything and everything in it. It allowed the user to work the magic that made up the place, and reuse that magic to any endeavor the wielder saw fit.

But its power was flawed. If the user still was 'bound' to another focus, the Keystone's power wasn't fully synced with the other person. And the imbalance would warp the holder, change them. Cendan paused and reread the last words. The Keystone would change him, permanently. Due to this, the Keystone had been locked up and away. Locked up from anyone trying to use it.

So that explained it. Marcus was till bound to his ring. The Keystone had to be used by itself, or it would warp and change the wielder. All their darkest thoughts and desires would be released; all those demons would surface. The jealousy that Marcus felt about Cendan had become overarching hate. The desire that he felt for Jasmine had become a dark craving to hurt her, to express power over her.

A madman with a magic stone that gave him total control over the place where Cendan was locked up. A madman who hated Cendan now with every part of his very soul. And a madman who, very likely, was watching and waiting to make his move. But why did he want me here Cendan wondered? While the information on the Keystone answered a great many questions, some it didn't. What was it that made Marcus want him here, besides hate? If it was as simple as that, Marcus would have attacked him and Heather as soon as they walked in.

No, there was something else going on. A growling stomach reminded Cendan that he hadn't eaten anything in hours. He was hungry, tired, and more than a little stressed out. He grabbed a journal for reading material, and headed towards the kitchen, keeping a grip on his focus the whole time. He was three corners away from the kitchen when Marcus stepped around the corner.

Chapter 22

Marcus. He looked terrible to Cendan's eyes. Thinner, approaching skeletal. His skin pulled tight against his bones. Scraggly patchy hair grew in around his face, his hair limp and greasy looking in the flickering light. He said nothing, starting at Cendan with a maniacal grin.

"Marcus. Nice to see you," Cendan said trying to stay calm. "I know what you have, Marcus. The Keystone. You need to understand; it's twisted you, it's unsafe..."

Marcus's hand shot forth holding a small stone sphere; the Keystone.

"Mine." Marcus growled and attacked. Cendan could see the torrents of magic flow off the Keystone and towards him. He pulled as much as he could into the wards he had set and steadied himself. He felt as if a giant wave had come and tried to knock him over. He stumbled, but didn't fall. Gasping for breath, Cendan held up a hand.

"Wait... Marcus..." Anger crossed the crazed face of Marcus. Why hadn't Cendan collapsed? Marcus struck again, and then again... Cendan didn't fall.

Cendan, for his part was barely holding on. Each wave seemed to come from everywhere, and he was having a hard time keeping his wards up. The only blessing he had was the fact that Marcus didn't really understand the power he had, or that he was using. Cendan was buffering his wards with the very same magic Marcus was using to attack him with! But being how Marcus didn't understand, and couldn't see the magic, he didn't know that.

It did not, however, make withstanding the attacks any easier. Each time Marcus tried to overwhelm him with magic, he had to fight, even scrabble to stay above it. He knew Marcus was trying to knock him out, and that was something he was not about to let happen. Each attack made Marcus angrier, however. As each one failed, the rage got closer to the surface.

"FALL!" Marcus screamed, as he threw the biggest attack yet.

Cendan stumbled to his knees, but still didn't fall. All his concentration kept on keeping his wards up. Finally, with an incoherent scream, Marcus charged him and swung the stone at his head. A sound like a bell went off as the sphere impacted on his last ward. Cendan fell at that, curling up into a fetal position on the floor. Marcus, however, felt like his head was being torn in two; one part the old Marcus, the other this new violent monster.

"Wha…" was all he could say for a second.

Staring at Cendan, his face retook the rictus of hate and he screamed before running away down the hall. Cendan sat up and pulled as much magic as he could into the wards. He didn't have a clue what to do about any of this, but at least he'd survived the initial attack. He hoped that fact would give Marcus pause and delay the next attempt, hopefully giving Heather and Jasmine the time they would need to get help.

Jasmine dried her hair as she stood in Cendan's living room, showered and full. Now, if she could only forget what Marcus had done to her. How had her oldest friend gone so crazy? Those thoughts, dreams… Jasmine shuddered at her memories. He'd never physically touched her, for that she was grateful, but things he had sent into her mind were worse than anything he could have done physically. All to get to Cendan, or get revenge on Cendan. Why did he want Cendan back so badly?

And now, here she was. Out. Away, and with Heather, the witch. Heather stood looking out the window, her hand turning that twisted wooden circle that she used. She turned to Jasmine, flashing her a fake smile.

"Jasmine, I... need to apologize. For the store, I mean. Before."

Jasmine simply nodded. That was nice at least.

"So what has happened since I was put under by Marcus?" Jasmine asked, keeping an eye on Heather. "I mean, it's obvious things have. And then we need to think about how we can help Cendan. Marcus is a crazy man. I won't leave Cendan there powerless."

Heather gave a real smile at that. "Oh, Cendan isn't powerless. In fact, Marcus is going to find it far harder to do anything to him than he expects. As for what's been going on, let me fill you in."

Jasmine listened in silence as Heather gave her a synopsis of everything that had happened with the Shrouded, only interrupting to make sure she had everything straight. So, Cendan had been getting a crash course in magical training, had nearly been betrayed by this Gardener person, and had to run from these Shrouded people. Shrouded. She had a hard time believing there was a whole secret group of people that the Bridgefinders didn't know about that could use magic.

Oh they'd known there were individuals here and there, but a whole magical secret society? Her doubt was met, however, with the apparent truthfulness of this by the mere fact of Heather's existence. Heather was far more than some crazy witch making deals with creatures of the Slyph. She had abilities that Jasmine didn't understand. And with great reluctance, she knew they were magic. Just as she knew whatever Marcus had done; that had been magic as well.

An edge of concern crept into her thoughts however, Heather and Cendan had spent the night here at Cendan's house? Why did she care about that? Cendan was a grown man, he could do what he wanted. He had saved her and she wanted him to be happy, but with this woman? This... witch? She had no claim on him, that was in the past, but still. Jasmine mentally shook herself, this wasn't the time to worry about this.

Her childhood training notwithstanding, it was obvious that magic was real, and that she and the other Bridgefinders could and were using magic. It was a strange thought, and one that deep down gave her a small thrill.

"So, Cendan... How do we get him out?" Jasmine asked point blank. "We will need him if there ever is an attack by Grellnot."

"We may, and just may be able to get in with outside help, but I'm not sure." Heather paused and held up her hand. "Do you feel that?" Screams erupted from outside as Heather and Jasmine ran outside. Bridges. Bridges everywhere. Creatures, the like that neither had ever seen, came rushing out mixed with things they had fought many a time.

"We need help!" Jasmine yelled as years of training took over. She was tired, and not really ready for this, but she was a Bridgefinder. This was her job! Heather stood and nodded. Her eyes closed and then opened.

"The Shrouded are coming to help!" Jasmine and Heather ran down to the nearest Bridge, and closed it, banishing creatures left and right.

"Too many!" Jasmine yelled. Heather nodded. This was madness. A man appeared nearby, with four others, all gasping. Heather recognized them all.

"Whoop! Help has arrived!" Heather yelled as she sent a goblin howling back through the nearest Bridge. Her elation was short lived, however. An attack of this scale could only mean one thing. Grellnot had won.

Across the city, The Shrouded responded. Fighting off creatures and sealing Bridges. They weren't Bridgefinders, and it took more of them to do it. They still, however, weren't willing to let Grellnot win. Many a small prayer of thanks was said to the EVA machine of the Bridgefinders', in contrast to their normal curses. The day would have been unwinnable if the bridges hadn't been contained.

As it was, they held their own for now. Though losses happened. A person here, a face there, broken by a lumbering giant. A young witch speared by a gremlin's poison tipped dart. But they held. But where was Grellnot? Where was the leader of this madness at?

A sound that shook his bones went off in the lair, forcing Cendan to steady himself. He had nearly knocked the plate onto the floor. That sound? What had that been? He took one last bite of his food, and raced toward EVA, the only place he knew of that could make something like that. It was an alarm, something was happening, something bad!

"EVA?" he reached out in his mind, pulling every ounce of spare strength into the message, trying to break through the fog that covered the link between him and the clockwork intelligence. Fear. Fear blossomed across the link. Fear and hate. Cendan immediately thought of Marcus; what was he doing? Bursting into the main room for EVA, however, everything looked the same as before. Still a mess, but nothing else. No damage; no new changes at all.

The sound went off again, nearly deafening him.

"EVA?" He tried to break through one last time. A glimpse of a face was all he got, but that glimpse was enough. Grellnot. Cendan's stomach fell, as fear rose. He worked to calm himself. There was only one answer for this, one reason. Grellnot had won. The Slyph, the threat that had motivated generations of Bridgefinders, was defeated. Knowing Grellnot, probably dead.

Grellnot now had the power of the Echo World, all the power. If EVA was sensing it, however, the chances were that Grellnot was attacking, and here he was, stuck in the Bridgefinders headquarters. Stuck with Marcus. He slammed his hand against the nearest wall. He shouldn't be in here. He should be out helping Jasmine, Heather, whoever else. He hoped the Shrouded would help, even in the face of the factions that wanted to end the Bridgefinders. Grellnot was a greater threat.

"Marcus! I know you can hear me. We have to get out, Grellnot has won. The Slyph is defeated! You know what Grellnot is capable of, you know its ways. We need to help!" Cendan yelled out, hoping Marcus was paying attention. "Marcus, this is crazy!" he called out again, but only got silence in return. Anger gave Cendan extra energy, and he ran towards the exit, determined to break out.

He threw everything he could at the transition point. Patterns that he didn't even know what they did, all to no avail. Unless Marcus let him out, he wasn't leaving. Which meant Jasmine, Heather, and anyone else were going to have to do this without him. Even worse, the everyday people, the 'normal' people, were going to die, get hurt, get scared and terrorized.

Cendan slumped down in the hallway. What did Marcus want? Why him? He'd attacked, but still never said what it was he wanted. What could he do? For once, Cendan had no answers. He was at a dead end branch and stuck.

Marcus raged in a forgotten back corner of the Garden. He'd had the traitor Cendan all to himself. No one to help him, no tricks, and yet he still couldn't destroy him! Somehow the fool had managed to withstand the Keystone. No one should be able to withstand the Keystone! Screaming and reaching out with his new power, He destroyed a swathe of vegetation, burning it down to the roots.

How? How had the traitor beaten him? He stopped and whirled around. He'd had help. He must have had help. That's it. That's the only way. Marcus was unstoppable here, but if Cendan Key had made a deal with the Slyph, given himself to her, her power might be enough to delay Marcus. That was it, Cendan was even more of a traitor. Now not just a betrayer of the Bridgefinders, but of the whole human race. The whole world!

Hate burned in Marcus. So if Cendan was working with the Slyph, then Marcus needed help too. Who could help him? Jasmine? No, she refused to see the truth. Ran from it. Stupid woman. Why didn't she see how much she meant to him? How important she was? Together they could have raised a new generation of Bridgefinders, challenged the Echo World itself! Instead, she'd chosen to turn her back on him.

He would get her back. Her escape had only been temporary. Her and that witch; what had they called her ... Heather? They would come back for Cendan. He knew it. Once they did, they'd fall back under his control. This time it would be different. This time Jasmine would love him. Heather would too. She was a witch, but still, they needed more Bridgefinders. They would both love him.

Marcus giggled as he stood; they would both be his. But first, Cendan Key. He needed that focus, he had to have it. Cendan must know about the lock, about the breaking of the bindings. That's why he kept it away from Marcus all those times, before Marcus knew the truth. Cendan had been in league with the Slyph even then, he was sure of it!

He needed an ally. Who could help him? Who hated the Slyph just as much as he did? Hated Cendan? The name came to him. It was obvious. Cendan reached out and lowered the barrier that kept the creatures of the Echo world out. There was only one ally, only one that he could use to rid himself of Cendan Key, forever.

Chapter 23

Grellnot ripped the throat out of a wizard, his claws bloody again. Grellnot roared with delight as it felt the magic leave the man in front of him. Grellnot feasted on the magic. It was all Grellnot wanted; it soothed its hunger if only for a moment. So hungry, so very hungry. Grellnot's creatures were dropping here and there, but Grellnot did not care.

Its creatures; their creatures. All were meat, and all were food to Grellnot. A long sniff and Grellnot whirled around. Grellnot wanted that stupid Maker. It had not forgotten the pain and embarrassment of failing to before. Not that Grellnot had cared what the Slyph had thought; Grellnot had been denied. Grellnot didn't like being denied.

Grellnot couldn't sense the Maker though. It could smell that other Bridgefinder, the woman one. And another woman, who smelled a bit like the Maker, but not exactly. The others, the Shrouded, Grellnot ignored. Grellnot had known of the Shrouded for years. Hiding things; silly humans. They were easy food for Grellnot.

Grellnot cast a wider net, still searching. Its hunger grumbled; always the hunger. A glimmer appeared in its awareness. Something was calling Grellnot. Peering with the sight, Grellnot saw an *in-between* place. A place Grellnot didn't know. The call came again. Wordless, but a call. Grellnot tried to ignore it, but the call became stronger.

"What do you want from Grellnot!" it screamed, holding its head.

The answer came quickly. Grellnot stood still and laughed. This place, this was where that stupid human Maker was hiding!

"You can't hide from Grellnot!" Dancing in a shuffling gait, Grellnot celebrated. Grellnot would end both the Slyph and the Maker the same day! It vanished, Grellnot's desire for revenge over riding its desire to kill for the moment.

Cendan stood slowly, feeling defeated. He hated this feeling. He normally knew what to do. He prided himself on finding a way, a path forward. Marcus hadn't beaten him in the sense of what he had tried to do earlier. But a stalemate, especially here, wasn't a winning proposition for Cendan. He didn't even know where Marcus was. That Keystone allowed him to hide anywhere in the place.

Worse yet, Grellnot had won. He was sure of it. Grellnot, with all the power it had, was a terrifying prospect.

"Marcus! We should be out there, defending our world. Not stuck in here, trapped. You swore to defend this world from the Echo world, from the creatures and plans of the Slyph! How is this doing that?" Cendan yelled out once more.

Silence greeted him, and the transition point remained quiet, blocked. Cendan was frustrated, and angry. Stalking his way back to the kitchen, he slumped down in a chair, unsure of what else he could do. He tried to calm himself and banish the emotions that were currently clouding his thoughts. Be logical he berated himself.

Firstly, he was trapped in the lair with Marcus. Marcus was over the top, totally insane. Marcus wanted something from him. He had no idea what. Grellnot had most likely won and was attacking the human world. Cendan couldn't leave because Marcus had effectively locked the door with that damned Keystone. Without the Keystone, Marcus wouldn't be able to stop him.

So he needed to know more about the Keystone. There had to be a way to stop it, destroy it, nullify it, something! He needed knowledge. And there was only one place he might get it, and that was in the Maker wing. Sitting here feeling sorry for himself wasn't going to get it done. Cendan stood and took off at a brisk pace. There had to be something there; anything would help.

Cendan was halfway to his goal when he heard it, a low throaty laugh; a laugh he'd heard only once before. A laugh that made him freeze. Grellnot. Grellnot was here! But where? And how? How could Grellnot have gotten in? Where was he? Cendan reached out with his sight; maybe Grellnot would show up somehow. His faith was well placed.

Grellnot was in the Garden! To his sight, Grellnot showed up as an empty hole, a space where magic seemed to flow in and vanish. Without considering any other options, Cendan sprinted to the Garden, bursting the doors open.

Grellnot stood over the bloodied body of Marcus.

"Stupid Finder. Bringing Grellnot here. Grellnot not help you!" it screamed at the still form. Grellnot raised its head and looked at Cendan. "Ah, the stupid human Maker. Grellnot find youuuu!" Its tongue reached out and licked blood off a long dirty claw. "Grellnot look for you. Grellnot search." Turning, the creature kicked the body of Marcus. "This one bring me here; this one think Grellnot help him kill you."

"Grellnot not need any help. Grellnot eat him, and Grellnot eat YOU!" Grellnot turned back to Cendan. "Do you know stupid human? Do you know what Grellnot has done?"

Cendan paused, trying to make sense of all this. Marcus had brought Grellnot here? To kill Cendan? That hadn't worked out for Marcus, apparently. Grellnot had attacked him the moment he'd gotten in.

"You uh ... defeated the Slyph?" Cendan asked, trying to bide some time while he thought of a plan.

"Defeat? Grellnot eat the Slyph!" the creature yelled back. "Eat her magic, her power. Grellnot has that power now. Grellnot rules the Echo World now!"

Cendan swallowed. The greatest fear they had thought of had happened. Grellnot, the walking thing of hunger, was now more powerful than it had ever been.

"Now, Grellnot, you know you can't hurt me…" Cendan stated, knowing that wasn't most likely true anymore.

Grellnot laughed again. "Stupid Maker. Grellnot could not hurt you before. But Grellnot is more now, Grellnot stronger now." Cendan looked at Grellnot, and could see just how true that was. While the magic didn't seem to flow inside the thing — that was where the near black hole of power was — the outside edge was alight with power. Threads thick and strong, interwoven with the points of light of the magic of this world. Magic that was the legacy of its hunts, all those Bridgefinders it had eaten, all that power it had absorbed.

Even by its creation, born of the mix of powers between the Slyph and the unwilling Oakheart. Grellnot was powered by both worlds. It had to be. Its existence owed itself to the fact that both worlds' power was used. If only there was a way to cut it off from one world, remove one world's magic…

Cendan paused. Rivenwood. His focus! What had the Shrouded told him? His focus had been Oakheart's. It was bonded to him now, but it had chunks of Oakheart's knowledge, his essence, embedded in the very metal it was made of. If Grellnot had been born of Oakheart and the Slyph's power, then maybe, just maybe…

He peered deeper at the thick corded magic that made up the outside of Grellnot. He didn't know what he was looking for, but this was his only chance. Grellnot was still watching him with an expression of anger, and he didn't know when the thing would leap. But out of the corner of his awareness, he saw it. The soft spot! That one speck, the one fuzzy little speck of magic. Could he do it? Could he unravel the very essence of Grellnot?

Grellnot spat. "Stupid human not talking. Maker up to something. Grellnot not give human that chance!" Cendan fell to one knee as he felt something pull at his soul. So like the first time he'd been attacked by this thing, but stronger, so much stronger. Pain shot through his head and chest, his hands grasping the air, trying to find purchase on something, anything to steady himself.

But if Grellnot was stronger, so was Cendan. Even with his recent fight with Marcus, he had been working on his defenses, working to buffer himself against magic. Grellnot could hurt him and hurt him badly. But he couldn't kill him, not this way. Slowly Cendan raised his head, teeth gritted to lock eyes with this demented creature. Grellnot spat and bit the air, frustration writ large. Cendan was defying the all-powerful Grellnot!

With a scream, Grellnot leapt, his hunger pushing him. Cendan had only a second to react but managed to grab his arms as Grellnot abandoned the magic attack and fell back to the physical. "Grellnot just kill you the old way." The thing said, its face inches from Cendan's. Its breath reeked of rot and mold, and older foul things. If he hadn't been so busy trying to stay alive Cendan would have retched his stomach out at the smell.

"GRELLNOT WILL WIN!" The scream came from his assailant, as Cendan felt his physical strength starting to weaken. While not exactly a weakling, he wasn't well versed in hand to hand combat with a short nearly demonic eating machine. He had to do something, and fast. He could feel Grellnot gather its power for another physical assault.

At that moment, Cendan reached out, and with all his strength, pulled the soft spot, yanking it out of the pattern. Pain. Pain like no other blew through Cendan. Heather had tried to warn him how much this hurt, but this was unlike anything he'd ever experienced. He could feel his mind twisting, stretching. His mouth opened to scream, but no sound emerged.

"Peace, Cendan Key." Sudden peace overcame him... That voice, was Oakheart's! "You have fulfilled my greatest wish; to see the end of my cursed child. The threat of Grellnot is over. I am just a wisp of a memory, a message left to see if it could happen." The pain left him as he watched Grellnot mid-leap. The threads of magic flittered off, unraveling.

Grellnot fell off of Cendan, screaming.

"Grellnot is all! Gellnot is power!" it screamed as it held itself. "What did the Maker do?" Grellnot yelled as it watched its power fall away, faster and faster. The very magic that made it fell into clumps, sloughed off and vanished. The magic that gave it life, drifting away.

"I unmade you Grellnot. I ripped the magic of my world out of you," Cendan said, his body tired, fighting off the exhaustion that threatened to overcome him. "You are gone."

Grellnot writhed on the floor, the pain of its unmaking too great to stand. Cendan watched as the magic left him, his power reducing faster and faster.

"Hunnnggrrryyy…" A whisper came from Grellnot, and then it was no more. A pile of greasy rags and the necklace of foci glinting in the light was all that was left. Cendan wanted to celebrate; he had ended the threat of Grellnot forever! His focus clattered to the floor, the sound of metal ringing in the empty space.

So tired. He reached out to grab something to steady himself, but blackness claimed him, and his body collapsed on the floor.

Marcus opened one eye. Grellnot's attack had not been unexpected, though the pain had been worse than Marcus had thought. Blood still seeped through the places Grellnot's claws had ripped. The Keystone had saved him, stopped Grellnot from eating him. He wasn't sure how.

Cendan had killed Grellnot; that was surprising.

"Still, even a traitor can do something useful sometimes," Marcus mumbled. Standing, he held his wound closed with one hand. Cendan still lived, he could see. "Not for long," Marcus said as he slowly made his way to Cendan's prone form. He kicked something on the floor and heard the ring of metal. The Key!

There the key! It must have fallen out of Cendan's grasp during the battle with Grellnot. Ignoring his pain, Marcus reached down and grabbed the precious thing. Marcus did not believe for a second that Grellnot had beaten the Slyph. There was only one way to end this. One way to make sure they were free forever of the danger of the Echo world.

Marcus would end this. Marcus would be the hero of the ages. Jasmine would come to him willingly. Everyone would know that Marcus, not Cendan, was the savior of the world! He kicked Cendan's form as he passed by, getting a small groan in response. Good. Marcus wasn't going to kill Cendan. He wanted him to know that he had won.

Marcus imagined Cendan's face, knowing that all his betrayals of the Bridgefinders, betrayals of the world, had gotten him nothing. Marcus would win. Marcus had won. Slowly he moved down the hall, blood dripping behind him. Grellnot's claws had worked into him deep, but Marcus had this job. To break the connection to the Echo world. Keep the earth safe.

Finally arriving at EVA's room, Marcus paused, trying to gather his strength. He drew in as much as he could; he only had a little father to go. The ladder was there, to the keyhole. The key would turn it and use EVA to break the bonds. EVA's voice came now, weak, but audible.

"Don't do this Marcus. It's a mistake."

Marcus snarled. "Don't talk back to me, machine. I will save us all."

EVA's voice continued. *"Do you know why Oakheart never used it? The key will destroy me. I will end. On top of it, breaking the binding between our world and the Echo world doesn't get rid of anything. It just means that instead of Bridges only being formed between our world and the Slyph's, it means Bridges can be formed from anywhere to here."*

"LIES!" Marcus yelled. "Oakheart was too weak to do this. Makers should never be given that much leeway. I will end this!"

Marcus started up the ladder, his bloodied hands slipping in places, unable to get a grip.

"Don't do this. Please I beg you!" EVA's voice came plaintive. *"We don't know what could be out there. The Bridges could lead to things far worse than the Slyph."*

As he climbed to the top, Marcus growled. "I don't want to hear any more of your lies!"

He took the key and placed it in the keyhole, making a soft click as it slid into place.

"I, Marcus Wheeldon, leader of the Bridgefinders, will now end this!" Marcus said proudly. He imagined himself standing before an adoring crowd, cheering for him. Jasmine at his side, his wife. He reached out and turned the key.

Chapter 24

Cendan awoke, opening his eyes to the sight of Heather standing over him, her face a mask of worry, sweat, blood, and dirt.

"Cendan! Are you ok?"

He could only nod in response. He hurt. Every scrap of him hurt.

"What happened?" Heather asked, helping him sit up.

"Grellnot... Gone. I... unmade him. I ended Oakheart's part of the pattern," Cendan mumbled. "Marcus let Grellnot in, to kill me. Grellnot killed Marcus, but I..." Cendan lapsed back into silence, the pain in his head pounding.

"Marcus didn't die," Heather said slowly. "He..."

Jasmine's voice came in now. "Marcus did something. I don't know what, but he did something."

Cendan raised his head. "What do you mean? His body is right..." Cendan pointed, but the body he expected was gone. "What..."

Heather slowly helped him up.

"Cendan. Do you remember what Rivenwood told you, about the Spinner? Valkith? Marcus... somehow... broke the bindings."

Jasmine shrugged. "I know nothing of that. But I know this; the moment Grellnot died, all the Bridges closed at once. What few creatures were left behind died, flopping in the sun. The Shrouded helped get rid of them. I think, I think we won."

Cendan rubbed his head. "We won?"

"Only sort of," Heather said. "The threat of the Slyph, the threat of Grellnot, those are gone. Even the threat of the Echo world; that's gone." Cendan felt a small smile build through the pain.

"Then we did win," he whispered.

"Cendan, listen. Marcus broke the bindings. The earth is now open to anything that can make a Bridge to it. We don't know what that could be; maybe nothing, maybe a thousand things. We don't know if they are friendly; we don't know if they make the Slyph and Grellnot look like a cartoon villain. We don't know."

Cendan held his head. "Why does my head hurt so much?" he mumbled.

Jasmine looked at him sadly. "Cendan. He... whatever he did, Marcus... he destroyed EVA. She's gone. The room is a wreck. Maybe you can fix her again, but…"

Cendan, with a start, realized she was right. The presence, even the muffled presence of EVA, was gone. Jasmine held out his focus, its metal bright in the light.

"This was in EVA's room."

Cendan held the key; its smooth presence calming him. EVA, gone? No. He would repair her. He wasn't going to let Marcus take that away from him! Marcus, where was Marcus?

"So, where is Marcus? I swear he was dead when I saw him here. Though, with the attack by Grellnot, I didn't check." Cendan winced; even talking didn't feel good.

Jasmine sighed. "We don't know. There was a trail of blood, his blood, from here to EVA's room. But after that?" She shrugged. "We didn't find his body."

Heather looked uncomfortable. "Cendan, Marcus broke the binding. He was there at ground zero. He was probably pulled apart into nothing by the resulting magic release."

Cendan glanced at her with barely open eyes.

"You used the word, probably. That's not making me feel better."

Cendan looked at his focus, trying to make sense of this all. They had won, but by winning they may have just opened themselves into new dangers, new threats. He raised his head, taking in the light of the Garden. The maybes would have to wait. For the moment, they'd won.

Sand crunched under his feet. The smell of the ocean brought a smile to his face. The human world once more. The human, Cendan, had been smarter than he'd thought. Fulfilling the letter of the bargain, but in such a way that he didn't think the Elves would get an advantage. But without the Slyph, without Grellnot, he, King Lachnin was the power on the Echo World. And there was so much to do.

What that Bridgefinder hadn't known, hadn't realized was this the Bridge he created to the Echo World, the Slyph's.... no he corrected himself, the ELVEN World, was protected from the cutting of the worlds from each other. This had always been a possibility though one that he had considered somewhat remote.

But now, here he was, King Lachnin of the Elves, ruler of their own Echo, possessing the one Bridge between their world and the Human world.

Putting them on an island was only a minor setback, one that they could overcome, given enough time. And time was something they had plenty of.

Printed in Great Britain
by Amazon

66257330R00139